STRAY DOGS

STRAY DOGS

Writing from the Other America

EDITED BY
WILLIAM HASTINGS

Down & Out Books
3959 Van Dyke Rd, Ste. 265
Lutz, FL 33558
www.DownAndOutBooks.com

Cover design by J.T. Lindroos

ISBN: 1937-4958-3-3

ISBN-13: 978-1-937495-83-1

Dedicated to the memory of
Charles Bowden and Johnny Winter.

CONTENTS

CONTENTS

Introduction
Lou Boxer

Better to seem to lose the battle and actually win, than to seem to win the battle and actually lose. Sometimes the seeming loser is in truth the victor. One must know the definition of victory before one engages the enemy.

—Sun Tzu, *The Art of War*

This book is not for the weak at heart or easily offended. *Stray Dogs* is a head-on collision with life. There are no airbags, safety glass or roll bars in this vehicle. The stories, poetry and lyrics that you will read and hear about are indeed closer than they appear in your side view mirror. For indeed the other America is our America. It is the home of fractured dreams and failed ambitions. It is war out there. Like it or not. The losers are the victors.

In a 1975 *Fiction! Interview* with Northern California novelists, Don Carpenter, author of *Hard Rain Falling*, was asked, "What does it take to be a good writer?"

His answer was a simple one: "Luck. Talent. Energy. Love. Madness. And the ability to throw your entire life away for what you want. Courage, in short." Add the necessary honesty and objectivity to deconstruct life to its stark, basic landscape and you are left with the brutal truth, beautifully rendered. No subterfuge. No innuendo.

All of these talented writers, poets and musicians

included in this collection are anything but stray dogs. They are more like free-range purveyors of our lives. Told with unabashed candidness, their talents are readily appreciated as one after the other demonstrates the principles that Don Carpenter used to judge a good writer. Make no mistake about this.

Writing from the other America, the marginalized, the discarded and the losers are given a voice that can be heard loud and clear by these talented writers. No matter if it is Vicky Hendrick's "M-F Dog," Eric Miles Williamson's "Some Get-Back," Willy Vlautin's "Lorna," Chris Offutt's "High Water Everywhere," Chris Hedges' "Remarks," Joseph D. Haske's "Smelt," Ron Cooper's "The Art of Carving," Michael Gill's "27 Trap," Patrick Michael Finn's "Where Cat Scratch and Happy Valley Meet," Daniel Woodrell's "Johanna Stull," Sherman Alexie's "One Stick Song," Mark Turcotte's "Road Noise," Larry Fondation's "Cross Dressing," Steven Huff's "An American Uncle," poetry by Esther Belin, lyrics by Dickey Betts and Jason Isbell, you will be left shaken, disturbed and wonderfully alive. Enjoy.

Ramblin' Man
Dickey Betts

Lord, I was born a ramblin' man
Trying to make a living and doing the best I can
When it's time for leaving
I hope you'll understand
I was born a rambling man

My father was a gambler down in Georgia
He wound up on the wrong end of a gun
I was born in the back seat of a Greyhound bus
Rolling down highway forty one

Lord, I was born a ramblin' man
Trying to make a living and doing the best I can
When it's time for leaving
I hope you'll understand
I was born a rambling man

I'm on my way to New Orleans this morning
Leaving out of Nashville, Tennessee
They're always having a good time down on the
Bayou, Lord
Them delta women think the world of me

Lord, I was born a ramblin' man
Trying to make a living and doing the best I can
When it's time for leaving
I hope you'll understand
I was born a rambling man

Lorna
Willy Vlautin

Lorna turned on the heat in the car and when she did Rolly sighed heavy and rolled down the window halfway. He was forty years old and thin, his face hollow but clean shaven. He was short and at one time stocky in build, but he had been losing weight. He'd grown up in Billings with three brothers and a sister. He joined the army when he was twenty and stayed in for eight years before becoming a long haul truck driver. Years passed before he got off the road and started falling apart outside of Phoenix where he met Lorna.

"I'm freezing," she said.

"Well, I'm hot," he said as he smoked a cigarette. His nose was running, he had a cold. He was wearing three shirts, a sweater, and a lined leather coat.

"You're not supposed to bundle up in the car."

"Says who?"

"Don't you remember when you were in school and the teacher said to take off your coat when you got back from recess?"

"I'm from Montana."

"How many shirts do you have on?"

"It's winter for Christ's sake."

"I'm really cold, Rolly."

"Fuck," he said and rolled up the window. "Are you happy?"

"I will be when I warm up."

He coughed and wiped his nose on his coat. "I'm

5

going to sweat to death and you'll probably still be cold."

"I'm starting to warm up," she said.

"Help me take off the coat."

"Why don't you just pull over?"

"If we pull over every twenty minutes, we're never going to get there."

"I can't help it if I can't piss in a bottle."

"When I was on the road, I never stopped and now we stop eight times an hour."

Lorna began laughing. Her brown hair was pulled back into a ponytail. She was only thirty-four years old but her face was as worn and weathered as an old woman's. Her eyes were caving back into her and her skin was beginning to go.

"I can drive with my legs," he said. "Just help me off with the coat."

She grabbed on the sleeve and he pulled his arm out. He got the coat off and she took it and threw it in the backseat. He turned the station on the radio and began going up and down the dial until he settled on a country station.

"The problem is we're going to break down, I know it."

"You've been saying that since we left Phoenix."

"Well, I'm sure of it now," he said.

"I hope it does after we visit then," she said. "Do you want an apple?"

"You're eating fruit now?" He moved his hand to the dash, to a pack of cigarettes. He took one and lit it. "You want one?"

"No," she said. "I'm trying to be good."

He started laughing.

"Don't laugh at me, I hate when you laugh at me." Lorna turned around and reached into the back and found a grocery sack sitting on the floor. She took an

6

apple from it and again sat in the front seat. She wiped the apple on her sweatshirt, took a mouthful, and chewed it. But the second bite left her right incisor in the skin. It took her a moment to realize what had happened but when she did she just looked at it and began quietly crying to herself.

Rolly smoked that cigarette and lit another. Lorna held the apple in her hand. She closed her eyes. She hadn't sleep in two days; she felt sleep near but it wouldn't come.

"Hey," he said.

She opened her eyes.

"You hear that?"

"Hear what?"

"A belt's about to give out."

"What does that mean?"

"Forget it." He put his cigarette out and looked over to her. "What the hell's going on? There's blood all over your mouth."

"I lost a tooth." She began sobbing.

"Jesus," he said. "Take this." He handed her a blue bandana he kept in his back pocket. She took it and wiped her mouth.

She began shaking her head side to side. "We should turn around."

"We only have a couple hours to Reno," he said. "We've been driving for two days and now you just want to give up?"

"How can I see her when I look like this?"

"You can't start that again. Anyway, we don't have the money to turn around."

"Then just kill me," she said softly. She looked out the window. "Please just kill me, Rolly."

"I'm not going to kill you so don't even start with that. How's the gum, is it still bleeding?"

"It's gushing out."

7

"Press the hanky into where the tooth was."

She folded the hanky and put it in her mouth. "U shud jus kell mee."

"Don't talk with that thing in your mouth."

Lorna cried harder. She began hitting her leg over and over with her free hand.

He grabbed her arm and stopped her. "We'll take a break," he said. "Lovelock's the next town. There's a casino there. Let's have a smoke right now and then get a couple drinks. We'll get you cleaned up and calmed down then we'll get to Reno and get a room. We're doing alright. If that guy you know really wants the bundle, then we'll have enough cash to float for a long time. Alright?"

"I don't think I can."

"You have to pull it together, okay?"

Lorna nodded. She looked in her purse and took out a glass pipe. She loaded it and handed it to Rolly. He put the pipe in his mouth and took the lighter off the dash and lit it. He drove with his legs and smoked. He blew the smoke at Lorna. She waited until he was done then took the pipe back and set it on her purse. She looked in the rearview and pulled the bandana away. The bleeding had stopped, but the space between her rotting teeth was there.

"Don't start," he said. "Just have a smoke."

Lorna took the pipe and loaded it and put it in her mouth.

They sat at a table in the back of Sturgeons Casino. Rolly drank a beer, smoked a cigarette, and watched the TV. When Lorna came back from the bathroom, he lit a new cigarette and handed it to her. He moved a rum and Coke in front of her. They stayed for two hours until she was so drunk she could barely walk.

He led her out to the car and helped her into the passenger seat. He got them on the road and Lorna loaded the pipe again and they drove into Reno.

They got a room at the 777 motel on Virginia Street and waited out the night awake. By morning Lorna was drinking beer and pacing around the small motel room while Rolly sat on the bed and watched TV. When noon came they ordered a pizza but they both only ate a slice. Rolly took a shower and put on clean clothes.

"So tell me one more time how you know this guy?"

"We worked together at Harrahs when I was a cocktail waitress. He was a bartender but he inherited money from his mother. He's rich, Rolly. And he's a real fiend. He wants to buy the entire five ounces. That's what he said when I talked to him. He's not a drug dealer, he's just a fag with money."

"You're sure?"

"I think so."

"What does that mean?"

"We were friends, I trust him. And like I said he's got a ton of money. I know that."

"And what kind rich gay guy has a name like Burl?"

"Like Burl Ives, his mother named him after Burl Ives."

"Who's Burl Ives?"

"He was the voice in the Christmas show," Lorna said and gave him the phone number written on a scrap piece of paper.

Rolly looked at her and shook his head but called the number. He spoke with the man and set up a meeting. He hung up and said, "Now call your brother."

"I can't," she whispered.

"You'll feel worse if you don't."

"I don't know," she said.

"Take a shower."

"I don't want to."

"You look like shit," he said. "Take a shower and change your clothes."

She nodded and went into the bathroom. She came out twenty minutes later with a towel wrapped around her. She stood in front of the mirror and dried her hair.

She dressed and put on makeup. Rolly loaded the pipe and she smoked from it and opened another beer and called her brother.

"It's me, Walt," she said with a failing timid voice.

"Where are you?"

"I'm in Reno."

"No shit," he said. "Are you going to stay?"

"No," she said. "I don't think so. Rolly just has business here."

"Who's Rolly?"

"He's my boyfriend," Lorna said. "I'm living with him outside of Phoenix."

"So you're doing alright?"

"I'm doing okay," she said. "I really am...I'm doing a lot better than I was." She paused and looked at Rolly. "How's Cora?" she whispered.

"She's fine, she's great."

"What's she like?"

"She's shy but she's starting doing pretty good in school. It was rough for her for a while but it seems better now...She's got a great sense of humor."

"I was shy, too."

"I know."

"You're a good brother, Walt."

"You sound like you're out of breathe."

"I'm just nervous."

"Hey, everything here is okay. I have a new job where I get benefits so she has health insurance. I opened a bank account in her name for college. I'm keeping my shit together for a change. I haven't had a drink in five months."

"That's really good of you, Walt," she said and tears welled in her eyes.

"Do you want to see her?"

"I'm not sure."

"Are you okay?"

"I'm trying, Walt."

"I know you are," he said.

"Maybe I should just say goodbye."

"Don't, Lorna. It's just me...Where are you staying?"

"A motel on Virginia."

"What motel?"

"I can't remember the name."

"What have you been up to?"

"Nothing, really."

"What kind of work are you doing?"

"Rolly takes care of me."

"What kind of work does Rolly do?"

"He was a trucker for a long time," Lorna said. She couldn't catch her breath. "Can you hold on?"

"Sure," he said.

She held the phone to her stomach. "I can't do it," she cried to Rolly.

"For fucksakes, Lorna, you can do it, just calm down." He pointed to her beer sitting on the bedside table. She took a long drink from it, tried to breathe, and put the phone back up to her ear. "Sorry about that, Walt."

"It's alright," he said. "I'm just walking to pick Cora up from school. I have a ways to go. I have time."

"Is she growing fast?"

"Really fast, you'll see. I bought a camera. I take a picture of her every week standing in front of the door. She looks different than she did six months ago. I'll bring the photos."

"I bet she's beautiful."

"She is...A couple weeks ago, for Easter, I hid a bunch of eggs around our place. She knew all my hiding spots. Some of which I thought were pretty good. Anyway, when you don't think she's listening she is. So she's pretty sharp, too."

"Did you put anything under her bed?"

"Yeah," he said and laughed. "I couldn't remember what Mom used to do so I just put five dollars and a chocolate bunny in a paper sack."

"She used to put three dollars inside a new pair of sneakers. Three dollars for the three months until summer. She'd put them under our beds. But five dollars and a chocolate bunny is perfect...I guess I should go."

"Don't go yet," he said.

"I ain't much anymore, Walt."

"I know you are having a hard time, but don't go."

"I wanted to see her so bad," she said and paused. She again tried to catch her breath. "I can't even begin to tell you how much I think about her. A moment doesn't go that she's not in my thoughts. But now I'm here and I just don't think I can do it."

"First thing to know is she's fine, she really is. She can read now, she reads to me at night."

"She does?"

"Come eat dinner with us and she'll show you. Bring your boyfriend. She'd love to see you. I would, too."

Lorna looked at Rolly who was watching TV and smoking a cigarette. She walked into the bathroom and shut the door.

"Do you have school pictures?"

"I'll get them for you tonight."

"I don't think I can do it tonight. I can't eat dinner with her, Walt."

"You can."

She sat down on the toilet seat and ran her hand through her hair. "Walt, do you remember the China Diner?"

"Sure," he said.

"We used to meet there a lot, do you remember?"

"Of course I remember. Do you want to meet there?"

"I was thinking maybe I could do that. If I can't then at least I can see her in the window. Will you sit by the window?"

"I'll sit by the window," Walt said. "Have you been taking care of yourself, Lorna?"

"No," she said.

"You're still partying?"

"Yes," she whispered full of tears.

"How's Phoenix?"

"Not so good, Walt."

"We're just staying at the Stardust, but you can always stay with us. You know that, right? You're always welcome."

"Thank you, Walt. Let me think about that, okay? You said you had a bank account set up for Cora. What's the account number? I'll start putting money in it."

"You don't have to do that."

"I want to, Walt. I have to do something. I have to try and help. I've done nothing but ruin her."

"Don't say that."

"It's true."

"I'll give you the number tonight."

"Please, Walt, do you have it on you? I'd really like to have it now."

"Hold on, it's in my wallet," Walt said and paused. She could hear him breathing and fumbling for it. "It's Nevada State Bank. Do you have a pen?"

"I'll remember."

"It's a long number."

"I'm always good at remembering numbers," she said.

Walt read off the account number. "You got it?"

"I got it," she said. "I better go now or I'll forget it."

"I love you, Lorna."

"I love you, too," she said. "Don't hate me, Walt."

"I don't hate you, I've never hated you. And Cora's fine, that's the main thing, right?"

"It is," she said. "I have to hang up now or I'll forget the number."

"The China Diner at 5:30. Can you make it?"

"I'll try. Can you give me the number one more time?"

"Maybe you should get a pen."

"I don't have a pen, Walt."

He read the account number to her again and she hung up the phone. She had her eyes closed and the number ran through her head. She stood up and walked back out to the main room.

"Do you have a pen?"

"Maybe in the car," Rolly said. The TV was off. He was putting on his shoes. There was a map laid out on the bed. Lorna emptied her purse out onto the floor but there wasn't a pen. She ran out of the room and down to the office and borrowed a pen and piece of paper. She stood under the fluorescent lights while an old Indian woman watched from behind the counter. She began writing numbers down. She got four of them when her mind failed her. She couldn't remember the rest and left the pen and paper on the counter.

She walked back to the room in tears. She couldn't do anything right.

Rolly was smoking from the pipe when she came in the room. He gave it to her and she smoked from it.

"He wants to meet at a place called Paradise Park. He says it's off Oddie Boulevard."

"I know where it is," she said and wiped her eyes. She found it on the map and told him how to get there.

"What did your brother say?"

"I'm going to meet them pretty soon. You can just drop me off downtown."

"This guy better be alright," Rolly said and put on his coat.

"He will be. He's just a queen who's got a lot of money. He won't do anything funny." But in truth she wasn't sure anymore. She wasn't sure about anything.

"Alright," Rolly said and put on his coat. "You look good and you're going to have a good time. Remember you get to see your daughter tonight."

"I know," she said.

Rolly left her in front of the closed down Fitzgerald casino and Lorna walked slowly up West Street. It was nearly dark when she came to the China Diner and saw Cora and Walt sitting near the window. She stood in the parking lot for a long time watching. Cora's hair was shorter, almost in a bob. Even from there she could see that her daughter had grown. Walt sat looking at his watch and then finally he got up and ordered food at the counter and sat back down. Cora had a backpack with her, she opened it, and began showing Walt things from it.

When their food came she watched them eat, watched how her daughter held her fork, the way she swung her feet back and forth beneath the table. She moved farther away and hid behind a truck when they walked out of the small restaurant. She watched Walt hold Cora's hand, and she could almost hear her daughter's voice as she followed them to the Stardust Motel.

They went up the stairs to the second floor. Walt unlocked the door and Cora went inside and he shut the door behind her. He stood against the rail on the second floor and looked out. He waved to Lorna as she stood across the street next to the closed down Sundowner casino and Lorna waved back to him.

"Lorna" was originally published by Tin House.

M-F Dog
Vicki Hendricks

The broiling Key West sun was setting as Bob and I strolled the dog down Duval Street, the heat slapping our faces between buildings when there were no high walls or borders of bougainvillea for shade. It was a climate ripe for jock itch.

I had gotten the dog in hopes of attracting girls up at OSU who were looking for the wholesome, sensitive kind of guy who would care for a puppy. A broken leg had ruined that strategy, so I graduated and moved to the island in the summer with Bob. Both of us worked as waiters, hoping to write best-selling fiction. Writing a novel had been another plan for attracting women—or a woman—but I'd pretty much given up on that idea, too.

The dog was no longer cuddly. However, he was beautiful, having reached an age when his muscles were well-developed, his purebred Doberman body sleek, and black eyes bright with mischief. His step was spirited with the adventure and cheer of an evening walk around town where everybody was his friend. He held his nose high, sniffing for cats and places to piss, his coat shining obsidian-black. Bob and I were less energetic. Sweat rimmed the necks of our T-shirts and rolled from between our shoulder blades to the waistbands of our shorts as we kept up his pace.

Key West was expensive, so we were renting a tiny, un-air-conditioned apartment made out of an old house that had been divided up. Bob had a girlfriend already—he always had one within days—a nice girl who spoiled him relentlessly. She waitressed at Louie's Backyard and had a small air-conditioned place with a pool where Bob usually stayed, rather than us taking turns between the bed and the couch. We would meet her at Louie's after work for a drink by the water.

I was unattached, as usual, alone. I'd always been weak in the knees around women, probably from needing somebody so badly, some connection to a female personality—sex—or even love. Normal women never liked me. I figured the dog would change that, but then I'd missed my window.

We decided to stop at the Iguana Cafe for a snack and a beer, where I could tie the dog in a shady spot on the sidewalk next to the table and feed him a bite of conch fritter or a shrimp tail now and then. He took things nice and slow from your hand. When we sat down, he cocked his head at Mr. Iggy in the cage behind us. Mr. Iggy turned his head and looked back—good attention skills for an iguana—and I was thinking the two might have some kind of inter-species understanding.

I looked at the cage and realized this reptile had his own name tag hanging right there, unoriginal as it might be, and I still hadn't picked a name for a dog over a year old. But there was something pure and true about calling him "the dog," almost Hemingwayesque, and I decided to keep it that way.

We ordered a couple of beers and appetizer samplers with the conch fritters and shrimp. I planned on a piece of key lime pie for dessert. We were killing time, or at least Bob was, waiting for his honey, while I was seriously looking for my honey, or sweetheart, or even a ball-buster, at this point. It had been so long since I'd been with a woman, I probably couldn't tell the difference. The dog was wagging and looking hopeful at each person who passed by, almost like he was trying to help, except he didn't discriminate between the girls and the boys. In Key West that's in no way unusual, but I was still holding out for female attention.

We drank our drafts and nodded at people who stopped to give the dog a pet. It was "Hemingway Days" week and we remarked on the huge number of white-bearded, beer-bellied, sweating, middle-aged men with their tolerant wives. There were a lot of compliments on the dog, and I said thanks, thanks, thanks, and felt proud that the scrawny pup I'd picked out at the Humane Society had grown into such a beauty. It said something for my powers of selection and care.

"Gawd damn, that's a motherfucking, good-looking dog." The words bellowed from the mouth of a tall, string bean of a guy in a backwards baseball cap. "A gawd-damned, motherfucking, good looking dog." He stooped low and scratched behind the dog's ears.

"Thanks. He's a good dog."

"He is, sure is. He's a motherfucking, good-looking, son of a bitch, and don't let anybody tell you otherwise." He stared at me with defiance, like I would be one to argue.

"Yeah, he's a nice dog."

The guy took the dog by his collar and buried his face in the dog's neck, and I could feel my lips move toward forming a word, but I held back. He murmured into the fur, "Gawd damn, motherfucking, good looking, gawd damn..."

I looked at Bob and we agreed with our eyes—here was one drunk redneck that we'd have been better off to avoid. But it was too late. He straightened up and sat down on the empty chair next to the dog, his fingers working hard behind the ears.

The dog tilted his snout at me, tongue hanging out the side, and those shining black eyes got rounder. I swear we were thinking the same damned thing—grin and bear it.

A laugh came from the next table. There was a pretty brunette with a nose ring watching the drunk manhandle my dog. Her pupils were so large and dark, they might have been dilated—like most of the eyes in Key West on an evening—but it didn't matter. I was ready to fall in and drown. She was braless under a thin sleeveless T-shirt cut off just beneath her tits, some lovely tan ribs showing above the table. I already wanted her for a lifetime. I wondered how she could have sat down and ordered without my noticing. I searched behind her for the guy that must be on his way from the restroom or buying a pack of cigarettes, but there was nobody, and no other drink on the table.

I wasn't sure why she was laughing, but I looked at her and laughed along, like I was having a grand time sitting there with the drunk, instead of being fucking annoyed. She winked and toasted the air in my direction and I almost lost my breath as I took in her beautiful teeth, two perfect dimples, and innocent eyes sparkling brighter than all the Key West stars, even when you're out on a boat.

I felt a thump on the table and went back to where I didn't want to be. The redneck was waving at the waitress behind the cash register who was either blind or ignoring him. "Gawd-damned, gawd-dog. What's it take to get a beer around here?" He whacked the table top with a broad motion and Bob and I both grabbed our glasses.

"I hear Captain Tony has a good band tonight,"

Bob said. "Maybe you'd have better luck over there."

The guy looked at Bob and ice crystals formed between them, fast, despite the tropical air. "What's a problem, buddy? You mind me sitting at your table? I only come to say what a motherfucking, good-looking dog your friend here's got. You have a problem with that?"

My stomach clenched. Bob had been a linebacker at OSU, although he spent all his time on the bench. His hands were on his thighs and his posture had a spring-loaded quality that looked like trouble in the making. The dog had gotten bored and curled himself on the concrete, rhythmically licking his balls. I pointed at him and leaned closer to the drunk. "Know why he does that?"

The guy looked at me like I was the one cruising with the lights on dim.

I decided not to give the punch line. I shrugged. "Just wondering if you knew." I heard the girl sputter into her beer and start laughing. It sounded like some beer might have come through her nose, but I didn't look. The drunk gave me a nasty, sick look.

I took the dog's leash and tugged him up. "I'm going to take the dog around the corner for a piss," I said to Bob. I turned and stopped, hoping like hell the drunk would follow and I could lose him and loop back before the girl got away. With any luck she had food coming.

The drunk looked at me dumbly. "Come on," I said, "He likes you. Let's take this motherfucker for a piss."

Once up, the dog pulled and I followed slowly. I was not about to take the guy by the hand, but finally he rose and stumbled after us. We walked around the block to a parking lot with a fringe of grass, and the dog raised his leg. I watched as he squirted the white parking stone, remembering when he used to squat and dribble, wishing he was still a pudgy and cute female attractant. The guy and I stood watching in silence while the dog finished and scratched the scrubby weeds. I motioned towards the Hog's Breath Saloon. "Hey, buddy, here's a few bucks. Get us a beer, would you?"

I pushed the money at him and he took it from my hand finally and bounced his head in a loose sort of yes. As soon as he had put one foot in front of the other, I took the dog and ran. His nails scraped as we took off across the sidewalk. When I got back to the table, Bob had finished up the appetizer plate. The other table was empty. All that in less than five minutes.

I was close to tears. "Where's the girl?" I asked Bob.

He looked to the side and around the cafe. "What girl?"

I didn't bother to answer. Sat down hard. Sweat was creating a prickly itch around my balls and I reached under the table and scratched. It was just like me, jumping up to save the day, when Bob could take care of himself perfectly well. A scuffle might have led to conversation. I'd let the woman of my dreams slip away. I gulped my beer. It was warm, as I deserved.

The sun had slunk below the buildings, and Bob suggested we walk the dog over to Mallory Dock. I agreed. The dog could sniff legs and enjoy all the petting while we celebrated the sunset by viewing braless women in T-shirts. Bob and I cut across the wide lot of tourists toward the silhouette of Will taking his nightly tightrope walk near the edge of the dock and some bruiser struggling in chains. Behind him the orange ball hung three-dimensional over the horizon. It was a sight, for sure, but I wondered how these guys could perform their acts night after steaming night. Some of them had been there for over twenty years—Will and the bagpipe player over thirty. The bagpiper had been wearing that heavy plaid skirt every night since the day I arrived. Poor sucker, but then he probably had a braless babe at home, like everybody did but me.

I had missed out on a real chance this time, since the girl had obviously enjoyed my sense of humor. Then it occurred to me—Key West was a small town, and she was dressed for a night out. There were a limited number of places where she could go, and I could rule out the gay bars and many others, considering her age and style. All I had to do was search. She was looking for company, and I had to find her before somebody else did.

From that thought on, I wanted to burrow through the crowd as quickly as possible and get back to the bars. I let the dog pick up speed, and he began pulling and winding around tourists. He was strong and I had to reel him in close to keep from leash-burning people's calves as he made his turns. Bob glanced at us with annoyance, but kept up and didn't comment. The dog whipped me around a card table set up for Tarot readings and nearly knocked it down. I grabbed a leg and steadied it, but the cards flew off. I bent to pick them up, trying to hold the dog with one hand and stack the cards on the asphalt with the other.

I glanced under the table at the pair of shorts above, some white, veined legs at my eye level. "Sorry, ma'am. So sorry. I hope I haven't mixed up your whole future."

I was wondering who would pay for this weird stuff anyway. I stood and stacked the cards in the center of the table. And there she was behind it—my fantasy princess, my nippled beauty, my only

23

possibility—reading cards for a lady in a sailor hat.

"Your dog is psychic," she said.

My mind did a quick turnabout and snapped into spiritual acceptance before my face could reveal any doubt. I succumbed to instant belief in animal communication and Tarot cards. I felt my consciousness spread to embrace karma, crystal balls, numerology and astrology, charms, tea leaves, aromatherapy, acupuncture, and angels. Especially angels. I was a believer.

The dog began to buck and nearly took the table over. I was yanked forward, cursing my former God, and the crowd surged together between me and the two women, like the Dead Sea joining. I was yanked forward in the direction opposite of where I desperately wanted to go. I had given him too much leash, so that he was able to lever off the legs of the tourists and zigzag through the crowd. I cursed myself for the ridiculous idea of adopting a dog to attract female companionship.

I stepped on feet and walloped into hips. With a frantic dodge and grab, I maneuvered so not to trip an old tourist couple as they made their slow, hot progress across the dock. "Sorry, sorry. Excuse me, sorry." I kept the apologies going, as I got the dog under control, but tears were behind my eyes, in fear that my female vision of all physical and spiritual desire would again not be around when I got back. Finally, there was a clearing in the crowd. I saw up ahead that the dog had been making a streak for the trained housecat act. Dominique had a black one poised to jump through the fiery hoop and the dog was mesmerized. We hadn't gone far, but the crowd was thick and I couldn't see through to the girl. Bob was nowhere. I stood there panting and the dog glanced at me, considering his next move. I gave the leash several turns in my hand, so I had his neck tight, and let go a few harsh words. I probably hurt his feelings, but I didn't care. I started back toward where the girl was.

"That's a mother-fucking, good looking dog."

I pivoted, still out of breath, expecting to see the drunk and wanting to pop him. It was a different guy, a big six-four, maybe two-hundred-and-fifty-pound kind of guy with big shoulders and long arms. He stooped and gave the dog some walloping hard pats on the back. I stood baffled at what it was all about, this dog again eliciting words of obscene praise.

A voice came from behind, and amazingly, my angel stepped out of the crowd. "Hey, take it easy, buddy," she yelled at the ape. "How would you like to be pounded on the back like that?"

"I'd like it fine. Here, girlie, I'll bend down so you can reach." He bent over, but the girl turned her back to him.

"The stars are lined up right tonight," she said, and I took that to mean she felt lucky to see me again. She laughed and her nose ring danced in the low rays of sun.

There were no stars yet, of course, and she could have been sarcastically referring to the weird repeated compliment on the dog, but I agreed.

She put out her closed fist over my hand. "You dropped your keys under my table." They fell into my palm, and I slipped them into the deep pocket of my shorts without breaking eye contact. Bob and I had left the key under the mat at home, but I wanted a reason to be indebted to her.

"Thank you. Thanks." I gulped some air. "Hope I didn't mess up your business."

She shrugged. "It's all fate, one way or another. I'm finished for the night." She smiled.

I nodded, saturated by her huge liquid eyes. The big guy was staring at me over her shoulder, drunk and working up an attitude. He was standing on the dog's leash. Key West was fucked sometimes. I didn't want to waste more precious minutes, and I didn't want him whacking on my dog again, either.

I looked around for something to distract him, but the square was a conglomeration of distractions so thick there was nothing outstanding to remark on. I decided to go for honesty.

"Buddy, all I want to do right now is take this beautiful woman for a walk down the street and say the nicest things in the world I can and hope that she wants to get to know me. I never had a chance with a girl like this in my life."

I didn't dare turn to see the look on her face. I knew I'd given out way too much information and she'd realize I was a putz and could never get a woman—all the rest of them knew something, so why should she waste her time?

The guy put his hands up flat on both sides of his head, like he was in a holdup, disarmed, and I saw that my words had magically hit on a male code that he could understand. "I need to take my dog with me." I pointed to the leash under his heavy boot, and he lifted it in an exaggerated move and stood there balancing. Just then the sun slipped beneath the water, and the nightly wave of applause rolled over the crowd. The guy bowed, taking credit for the beauty of the universe. I put my arm around the girl and turned, letting out a grateful breath, and we both followed the dog away from the dock, winding through inebriated tourists.

When we got back to her table, I folded up the legs and stuck it under my arm. She said she lived on Eden Street and took the leash from my other hand and walked the dog, who had finally worn down. I tried to set a slow pace beside her, dreading when she would say thank you at the doorstep, and it would all be over.

It was a short walk, very short. I propped the table against the porch rail and she passed me the leash and stood there, a one-second hesitation. I saw the word "Thanks" forming on her mouth in slow motion and her tongue touch her teeth, "Th—"

"Can I buy you a beer at The Bull?" I said it too fast, like the classic dickhead I was.

She chewed her lip. "Okay."

I told her I was Lenny, and the beautiful name Alcira flowed from her lips.

As the night cooled and the smell of jasmine took over the atmosphere, we walked down the cracked sidewalks, stepping over roots and ducking under low-hanging trees and bushes together. We passed under a balcony, where the scent of weed mingled with the perfume of the flowers, and she said something about drugs in Key West, but I missed it. My ears had turned themselves off as my eyes became magnets to her lips, the plumpness, softness, the way they moved across her teeth when she spoke. I didn't even mind the nose ring.

We stopped outside The Bull and I looked for a place to tie the dog. Hard rock, the musty smell of old beer, and an overflow of bikers poured from the open doors and floor-to-ceiling windows. I pointed ahead, and we looked at each other and continued walking.

"Let's pass on that place. I've got stuff at home," I said, feeling brave in the drunken evening air. We strolled away from the crowd to where the sidewalks were cracked and the houses needed paint, my neighborhood. I walked Alcira across the dingy wooden porch and reached under the mat for my key, hoping she wouldn't notice, and wondering how long I could keep her there. I put the dog out back, brought her a beer and sat down next to her on the ugly green couch, roach-burned by former tenants, thinking I should have tossed a sheet over it.

She took a few sips from her bottle, then rose and slipped onto my lap like a cat. My arms went around her and my mouth to her throat. It was so easy. I heard her set the beer on the glass-topped end table.

"What else you got?" she asked.

"Uh, wine?"

"I hoped maybe you'd have a little X. I'm coming down."

"Sorry, no."

"Grass?"

"Sorry. But I don't mind if you smoke."

"Didn't bring any."

I was probably one of the few guys living in Key West without some sort of stash. It struck me that I wasn't her usual type, but I started kissing her neck again, ferocious yet tender, and after a few seconds she settled against me and began to tongue my ear.

Suddenly the dog became loud out in the yard, as if he knew I was finally getting some. Did he realize I was responsible for having him neutered? As my mouth went hard over Alcira's, the bastard hit a high-pitched yelp that cut like nails.

Then came the neighbor's guttural blast, almost as loud as the barking: "Fuck dis, mon! Shut dat motherfuckin dog up! Shut it the fuck up!" A door slammed.

There was silence for an instant and I felt something break, the spell of the night. I tried not to know it. The dog started up. Alcira drew back and looked me in the eye. I knew I should go out and bring in the dog, but I held on, praying for calm.

"That mother-fucking dog," I said.

We both began to laugh. We shook and howled and guffawed, holding each other by the shoulders, until all the loneliness of my lifetime tumbled down and disappeared between the cushions of the ugly couch, like small change. We couldn't stop snuffling and snorting, and the sounds of our laughter sent us into high abandon. She yanked off her shirt—as if it would help her breathe—her tits bursting out like sunset from under a cloud, her flushed nipples erect and magnetized toward my mouth. She draped herself over me and I dragged my lips over her chest, tasting her sweet saltiness. I began to believe that I did owe that mother-fucking dog something. I owed something somewhere.

Until the dog started barking again, I hadn't realized he had stopped. I buried my ears in Alcira's soft breasts and ignored him. He got louder and more irritating. I could picture him out there, his head and shoulders aimed at the door, ribs expanding and then his diaphragm punching out the air, all his energy forced into his lungs and throat. His ego was hurt. All night he'd been a star until I locked him in the backyard.

There were footsteps on the porch. Somebody stopped outside the screen door, on the other side of the wall next to us.

"Shut dat mother-fucking dog up." It was almost loud enough to rattle our beer bottles on the glass table.

I took Alcira's head in my hands and she steadied and stayed quiet. The dog was woofing wildly out back. Alcira's huge pupils shone. It was the two of us and the dog against all the assholes in the world. I thought of letting the dog in through the kitchen and out the front, but I was afraid I would lose him. I stood up to face the fucker on the porch.

Something banged the doorframe. "Hey, mon, I know you're in dere."

The latch wasn't even on. I stepped to the door and my eyes stared straight into a bare tan torso, a washboard if I'd ever seen one, then moved up huge shoulders to white teeth in a smooth coffee face and long floating dreadlocks nearly touching the porch roof.

"What can I do for you?" I said. I expected him to fling open the door, stoop, and grab me by the neck.

"Look, mon, I'm tryin to get my little high on, and your fuckin dog is—" He stopped, his eyes looking over my head.

I turned to see Alcira pulling down her shirt behind me and wondered if she'd shown a flash of tit. Her nipples were big as peanuts under the thin cotton.

"Sorry," I said to the guy. I was about to use the same pity line that had worked at the sunset, but I'd lost Mr. Dread's attention. I wondered if a rough tap on his chest would be helpful, but my hand didn't move.

Alcira was beside me at the screen. "You got a nice fat splif over there, mon?"

"Oh, yeah, I surely do, girlie. Surely, I do."

The next few seconds passed in a blur of shadow, a touch of breeze. Through my haze of disappointment I felt, more than saw, the door opening and Alcira passing by, the glint of nose ring as she turned and smiled, his arm going around her shoulder. Footsteps trickled down the porch, and I thought how light on his feet this Jamaican was for such a big man.

As I walked through the living room to let in the dog, Alcira's abandoned beer caught my eye and I picked it up and drained it. My companion for the night was worn out and dropped down on the terrazzo. I started to hate myself for not letting him in when he belted out that first bark... or not nailing the Jamaican, a number of errors. The dog raised his head and nuzzled my hand, and I thought how lucky I was. He was a mother-fucking beauty, smart—and loyal. I was glad I'd waited to name him until I appreciated the depth of his soul.

"M-F Dog" first appeared in *Florida Gothic Stories*, edited by Anne Petty, published by Kitsune Books, May 2010.

Goddamn Lonely Love
Jason Isbell

I got green and I got blues
And everyday there's a little less difference between
the two.
So I belly-up and disappear.
Well I ain't really drowning 'cause I see the beach
from here.

I could take a Greyhound home but when I got there
it'd be gone
Along with everything a home is made up of.
So I'll take two of what you're having and I'll take all
of what you got
To kill this goddamn lonely, goddamn lonely love.

Sister, listen to what your daddy says.
Don't be ashamed of things that hide behind your
dress.
Belly-up and arch your back.
Well I ain't really falling asleep; I'm fading to black.

You could come to me by plane, but that wouldn't be
the same
As that old motel room in Texarkana was.
So I'll take two of what you're having and I'll take all
of what you got
To kill this goddamn lonely, goddamn lonely love.

Stop me if you've heard this one before:
A man walks into a bar and leaves before his ashes hit the floor.
Stop me if I ever get that far.
The sun's a desperate star that burns like every single one before.
And I could find another dream,
One that keeps me warm and clean
But I ain't dreamin' anymore, I'm waking up.
So I'll take two of what you're having and I'll take everything you got
To kill this goddamn lonely, goddamn lonely love.

Tour of Duty
Jason Isbell

I'm arriving on the day's last train.
Stepping on the platform, trying to see you through
the rain.
I don't know the ways you've changed since I left,
and I really don't care.
I've done my tour of duty now I'm home and I ain't
going anywhere.

I taught myself to tolerate the pain,
all the loneliness and boredom and the work I did in
vain.
All the work we did in vain. Now I'm not the same as
I was.
I've done my tour of duty now I'll try to do what a
civilian does.

I promise not to bore you with my stories.
I promise not to scare you with my tears.
I never would exaggerate the glory.
I'll seem so satisfied here.

I've been eating like I'm out on bail.
Collard greens and chicken wings and oysters by the
pail.
Eating oysters by the pail, making up for those lost
days.
I've done my tour of duty now I'm going to put you in
the family way.

We'll laugh like little children telling secrets.
Probably cry like old women drinking gin,
because I've done my tour of duty now I'm home
and I ain't leaving here again.

I've done my tour of duty now I'm home and I ain't
leaving here again.

High Water Everywhere
Chris Offutt

Zules drove slowly, the headlights of his eighteen-wheeler dull against the fog. He'd driven in rain for two days, and it was hard to know where the road left off and the land began. The moon and stars were gone. He was running heavy through Oregon, following the Lower Callapooya River to avoid weigh stations on the interstate.

Over the trucker's channel came a report that a dike had broken. Zules switched to the local police band and heard a cop's voice telling emergency workers to evacuate immediately. The river wasn't just spilling over the top of the dike. Pressure had torn a hole through a weak spot and water was surging across the bottomland.

Zules steered to the shoulder and stepped out of the truck. Blown rain stung his face and arms. He cranked down the trailer legs and unscrewed the hoses that held the brake and electric lines. He worked fast, smashing a finger in the darkness, paying no more attention than if he'd nicked the handle of a tool. He didn't feel right about leaving his load, but without its extra weight he could beat the coming water. He climbed into his truck and pushed hard through the gears. The land reminded him of a tabletop, and he was heading for its edge.

When he reached a roadblock manned by a state trooper, he knew he'd outrun the river gushing through the dike. Zules slipped his hand into his shirt pocket and touched the small gourd his mother had given him for luck. It was dry.

He drove to Crawfordsville, got a room, and reported his abandoned trailer to the county sheriff.

Zules was so tired he was wide awake. He went to the motel lounge and ordered bourbon and branch. The only customer was a woman slumped at the bar with her eyes closed, both hands around an empty glass. She lifted her head.

"Don't mean to bother you," Zules said.

"You didn't," she said. "I was just testing my eyelids for light leaks."

Zules told her about losing his trailer. She listened as if his story were common. Her clothes were wet and muddy.

"It rained every day for two months," she said. "Then started raining twice a day. The clear-cut let the water run off the mountain. This whole town's on one slow drown. I'm sick to death of it. My store's got four feet of water in it."

"What kind of store?"

"Frame shop. The wallboard leached the water to the ceiling till it fell in. The light fixtures electrocuted the water snakes. They're still floating on top."

She laughed without changing her eyes or her mouth. It was just a sound coming from her head.

"I cut through here to dodge the flooding," Zules said. "All I had to do was make California and I'd be safe."

"Water runs south."

"I damn sure wish I never."

"I got wishes, too."

"Who don't."

"Not like mine," she said. "I wish I was somebody else. I'm not a good person anymore."

"Maybe you're a little drunk's all."

"I can hold my liquor."

"I ain't saying you can't."

"It's the water," she said. "We don't have anywhere to put it. It won't pile up like snow. It just stays and then it goes bad. Same as me."

"Maybe you should have some coffee."

She stood and leaned against the table.

"I'm not drunk," she said. "I'm sober as a judge."

"That ain't saying much where I'm from."

"Maybe you should have stayed there."

The woman walked slowly to the door, taking each step in a careful manner, resting her hand on bar stools for support. Zules wished he was the kind of guy who'd follow her home. He ordered another shot. He couldn't quite believe that he'd abandoned a full trailer in Oregon. He felt like a turtle who'd run off and left his shell.

In the morning his head hurt. He turned on the TV and learned that a six-foot wave of water had ripped across the valley. The water had spread over the land like batter in a skillet, covering everything, moving on its own. The phone rang and Zules hoped it was the woman from the night before.

"This is Deputy Terry," a hurried voice said. "We got us a trailer. You'll have to describe yours."

"It's a Peterbilt. Grey and white with Kentucky plates. Mud flaps got chrome bulldogs on them."

"Son of a bitch. We got somebody else's rig."

"Regular yard sale out there, ain't it."

The deputy hung up and Zules went to the lounge, suddenly homesick for Kentucky. The hillsides were so steep it was like living in a maze, but it wasn't a place where you could lose a truck trailer. When Zules was home he stayed with his mother, who was seventy-four. As the youngest child, he was supposed to take care of her, but after a few days he'd be restless, ready for straight roads and flat land. His mother said he was like a cat that hadn't been neutered. He said she had a heart like railroad steel.

The TV in the bar requested volunteers to help sandbag the town, and the bartender offered Zules a lift. They drove through streets of water past floating propane tanks tied to trees. Sandbags made walls around buildings—the fancier the business, the higher the wall.

A dull gray sky covered the sun. Zules waded to a line of people passing sandbags. He found a shovel and someone squatted before him with an open bag and he filled it with sand. The damp air was heavy in his lungs. Shrubs were dead from too much rain. A man carrying a video camera with a number three on it stepped around the pile of sand. Beside him was a young man with makeup on his face who wore a fly-fishing vest and a duck hunting cap. He was talking into a microphone.

When the sand ran out, Zules walked through drizzle to a water cooler on the back of a National Guard truck. Soldiers in camouflage held walkie-talkies and damp cigarettes. The deputy sheriff was with them and Zules asked about his trailer.

"Nothing," the deputy said. He spat between his teeth, using a technique that Zules remembered practicing as a boy. "You didn't see anybody by that dike last night, did you? No hitchhikers or nothing?"

"It was hard to see," Zules said. "Why?"

"Somebody went up there last night and blew that stinking dike open."

"How come?"

"Give that water somewhere to go. It flooded ten thousand acres of cropland. Whoever it was didn't want that river to bust through down here."

"Hell, that's probably everybody, ain't it."

"You're the only man I know who was up by the dike last night."

Zules laughed until he saw the man's face harden.

"A farmer drowned," the deputy said. "You're the only man thinks that funny."

"I wasn't laughing at him," Zules said. "I was laughing at you thinking I'd flood my own rig. Ask your state trooper where I come on him. Here I bust my hind end moving sand for your town and you say I'm flooding it. I don't see you doing any shovel work. Your boots ain't even wet."

"Keep it up, son," the deputy said. "Run that mouth and see where you end up at."

"You can't lock a man up for talking. This is America if you didn't know it."

"It's Oregon and I'm the law."

"Damn good thing crime's low."

The deputy's face turned red. The National Guard glanced at each other, trying to hold back grins. The deputy reached for his handcuffs.

"All right," he said. "Let's go."

"I ain't done a thing," Zules said.

The deputy stepped behind him and slid the cuffs over each wrist, squeezing them hard against the bone. He moved Zules through ankle-deep water to a patrol car.

"Hey!" Zules yelled. "Hey, channel three! Here's some news!"

"Shut the hell up," the deputy said.

The camera man began to trot toward Zules and the deputy. Behind him came the man in the fly-fishing vest. He held the microphone over his head like a pistol. A ring of people stood quietly in the dark water. Zules saw the woman from the bar. She had her hands on her hips, glaring at the deputy. She looked better in the day, the opposite of most women Zules had met in a tavern.

"Officer," the reporter said. "What exactly—"

"Yes," the woman from the bar said. "Just what the hell do you think you're doing, Kenneth?"

The deputy began moving Zules to the police car. The backseat was bare metal with no door handle, and Zules slumped low to avoid leaning on his cuffed hands. He hoped the video footage stayed on local stations. He'd hate for his mother to see it.

Half an hour later, Zules was sitting in the county jail's common room, watching a television bolted high on the wall. Below it was a pay phone that didn't work. The other prisoner had the TV remote in his shirt pocket and a toothbrush in his mouth. He introduced himself as Sheetrock James, kin to Jesse. His hands were small, with the shortest fingers Zules had ever seen. The ends were chewed so badly that the nails were tiny spots surrounded by raw skin. His crime was wrecking a dump truck at a landfill.

"Best thing was me getting arrested," he said around the toothbrush. "I'm staying right here till the flood's over. How high's that water getting to be? You ain't in here on murder, are you?"

Zules shook his head. A soap opera was playing on TV, what his mother called "the stories." His mother never talked about neighbors, but gossiped about TV characters in an intimate way.

"Hey," Zules said to Sheetrock. "Your mama watch TV shows like this?"

"Ain't got one."

"No TV?"

"Mama," Sheetrock said. "I mean I was born from one. Just that she died when I was two. My daddy shot her. She was holding me on the porch, and he shot her twice. They say she set down easy to not let me fall. Daddy, he got twelve years over it. Then he went back to Oklahoma."

Sheetrock's voice was casual, as if he were discussing an afternoon of errands. Zules regretted that he'd started talking. He'd been in jail before and the best way to get through it was with silence, the same at his mother's house.

"Wake me up when the news comes on," he said.

"Sure thing, man. No problem. You must be one of those people who can take naps. I wish I was. I'm up half the night. It's like I can hear myself talk in my own head."

"Hush, now."

"Yeah, man. Sure. If anyone else comes in, I'll tell them to be quiet."

Zules closed his eyes. When Sheetrock started yelling, Zules knew he'd been asleep. For a few seconds he was disoriented, until the slow realization that he had awakened in a cage. It was a terrible feeling.

"Hey, man, it's you!" Sheetrock was pointing at the TV. "You're a goddam star. Look."

The reporter said that a trucker had been arrested for blowing the dike. There was a final shot of Zules in the back of the police car. Zules had never seen himself on camera and didn't care for his appearance. He looked rough, like someone from the worst hollows at home, a man who belonged in the back of a police car.

"Just think of it," Sheetrock said. "Me celling with a hardcase. I never knew nobody on TV before." He offered Zules the remote. "Here, wish I had more to give."

Zules waved it away and fought down the urge to pace. He didn't mind getting locked up and he didn't really blame the sheriff. Cops were just guys doing a job. Zules couldn't think of much worse work except maybe driving truck.

The jailer brought two trays of food into the common room. He gave Zules a hard stare and left. Zules ate the sandwich of baloney on white bread. A paper cup held boiled cauliflower. He gave his piece of cake to Sheetrock.

"Thanks, man," Sheetrock said, "Guess you're watching your weight, huh. What I wouldn't give for a pork chop right now. The water done jumped through this town, man. Worst flooding ever. TV preacher said God did it on account of Portland's porn shops."

The jailer came back with his mouth tight. Sheetrock started eating faster.

"Take your time," the jailer said. "Your cellie here's out. Somebody paid his damn bail."

Zules looked at Sheetrock as if seeing him for the first time. His clothes didn't fit and he needed a haircut. The toothbrush stuck out of his mouth like a handle as he ate.

"Want me to see about you getting out?" Zules said. "Bail can't be all that high on a car wreck."

"Nope. I'm a stayer. That water is bad for my nerves. It won't get in here, either. These cells are on the second floor up. Best place to be just now."

"I could bring you something."

"I got everything I want right here, man. You ought to stay, too. Lot to be said for a man who stays put."

The jailer led Zules to an office where he signed a form to get his wallet, keys, and the gourd. He figured the news had gone national and somebody at home had seen it. He was surprised they'd got him out so fast.

"Who paid my bail?" he said.

"Somebody went through a town lawyer." The

jailer opened the main door. "Come back now," he said.

Outside it was dusk and raining again. The water table was above the ground with nowhere to go and Zules felt caught in a crossfire from above and below. He'd heard that there was no new water in the world, that it was all a million years old, evaporating and coming back as rain. He wondered where the hole was that was left by the storms. Maybe the oceans were lower.

A car slowed behind him. The woman from the bar opened the passenger door and he got into the car. She wore a long vinyl poncho. Her bare legs ran into heavy galoshes.

"Are you hungry?" she said.

"Yes, but I don't much feel like eating."

"How was it?"

"Not bad. They got cable in there. They had that at home, half the boys would get locked up just to watch their shows."

"Where's home?"

"Kentucky."

"What part?"

"The part people leave. You from herebouts?"

"Born and bred, except for five years in school at Corvallis. Halfway through I changed my major from art to science. My whole worldview went from the right hemisphere of my brain to the left, just like that."

Zules nodded. He didn't know what she was talking about.

"Sometimes I feel like an English novel translated into Chinese. It's backwards and upside down, and you read it in the opposite direction. Know what I mean?"

He nodded again. People who'd gone to college

made him nervous. He always felt as if they looked down on him, were waiting for a chance to make him sound stupid. He'd learned to be quiet around them, and eventually he discovered that his silence made them nervous.

She pulled into a driveway and shut off the engine and got out of the car. Zules followed her. The small house was jammed with boxes stacked on furniture. Everything was off the floor. She pulled a bottle of vodka from a cabinet and poured two shots.

"Mi casa es tu casa," she said.

She swallowed the vodka and filled the glass again. Zules sipped his drink, wondering if what she'd said was from that backward Chinese book.

She opened a door and went down wooden steps and Zules followed. Water was seeping along cracks in the basement walls. An arched stream spouted from the corner like a fountain. Several inches of water ran steadily across the floor toward a large hole in the corner. She shoved a stick into the hole. There was a dull click and the sound of a motor.

"Sump pumps got a short," she said.

"Kindly risky in all this wet."

"It's what I'm down to for risks. I have to start a bad habit just to have one to quit."

"I gave up smokes."

"Me, too. Plus pot, the dog track, and demolition derbies. The older I get, the harder it is not to be bored. Travel does it for you, I guess."

"Well, I'm in new places pretty regular."

"Must be nice."

"Don't reckon," he said. "Once you leave a place, you're sort of plowed under for living there again. I don't stay nowhere but the truck mostly."

"I shouldn't have come back here after school. I guess that's what ruined me."

"You don't look all that ruint."

"I figure guys like you have every kind of connection."

"Well, I got cousins all through Ohio."

"That's not what I meant."

Zules nodded, glad that the basement was dark and she couldn't see his face turning red. She stepped close to him.

"You know why I wear a wedding ring?" she said.

"No."

"To remind me not to sleep with married men."

"I ain't married."

She kissed him and he could taste the vodka. Her poncho squeaked. She went up stone steps to a tornado hatch and pushed it open. Warm air blew into the cellar. Zules climbed the steps to a backyard where lilac bushes grew lush from three months of rain. The storm hid the stars. The sound of thunder spread across the night.

A quick gust jerked the woman's poncho and he could see the pale flash of skin. She took his hand and tugged him to the middle of the yard and kissed him. He smelled the lilacs and the rain. She began to unbuckle his belt. He slid his hands beneath her poncho and was astonished to realize that she was naked. Her skin was wet. The storm pelted them with water. Wind lifted the poncho and she tugged it over her head and it disappeared into the darkness as if yanked by a rope. Very slowly they sank to the ground. The earth was soft. She rolled him on his back.

Rain ran into Zules's mouth and his eyes and his nose. He no longer knew where the water ended and the earth began. The storm crossed overhead, rain flying in all directions, the bellow of thunder within each drop. From a long ways away he could hear someone yelling. The sky was black and the air was warm. The yelling voice became his own. As soon as he recognized it, he stopped. In a quick flash of lightning he saw her above him, her arched body streaming water, her face aimed at the sky, the veins straining in her neck. She resembled someone fighting not to drown.

The storm moved rapidly east, leaving a drizzle that tapered away. High in the night, a speck soon became one of many stars. He felt her breathing become normal. His mind relaxed, moving in various directions at once. He thought of her basement, which reminded him of jail, and he realized that she'd been waiting for him on the street.

"Was it you who bailed me out?" he said.

"You guessed."

"How much it run you?"

"Six."

"I can't pay you back anywhere soon."

"That's not important."

"What'd you do it for?"

She didn't say anything.

"Not for this," he said. "You didn't get me out just to bring me here, did you?"

"No. I'm not that hard up."

"Well, why then?"

"That deputy hasn't slept in three days. The flood's just too big for him. Sort of over his head. You're the first person he saw all summer that he didn't have a history with. He's not really that mean."

"Sounds like you know him pretty good."

"He's my brother."

Zules became tense, aware that the air had turned chilly and he was lying in mud. Kentucky had high ground, woods to hide in, and thousands of creeks to drain the water. When he was home, he felt smothered by hills. Now he was trapped by flood. He'd been safer in jail. A part of him envied Sheetrock for knowing exactly what he wanted. Zules chuckled.

"What?" she said.

"Nothing. Just a guy in jail."

"It should be me."

"You wouldn't like it."

"Maybe not," she said. "But I'm guilty."

"Everyone is of something."

"I mean really guilty."

"You don't have to tell me nothing."

"It was me who blew that dike."

She began to cry and he held her.

"I thought it would take the pressure off down here," she said. "You know, save the town from getting flooded out. I wanted to help people, but that man died. It's the same as if I killed him."

Zules gave the woman a long, tight hug and gently lifted her off him. She was shivering. Her wet hair made her head look small. He led her into the house and poured vodka, which seemed to revive her. Water pooled on the floor where they stood. Zules closed his pants and buckled his belt, feeling awkward since she was naked. A mosquito hummed past his ear. He wanted to say something but didn't know what. She spoke instead.

"You just go around living however you want. Must be nice to be that free."

"Except when I get thrown in jail."

"That's all this town is. One big jail of water."

Zules slid his hand in his pocket and offered her the little gourd. The seeds rattled. She held it in cupped hands, dripping water.

"For luck," he said.

"I hurt all over."

"I know."

"There's no need to stay," she said, "or go."

He wondered what she wanted but didn't know how to find out. He moved to the door, still looking at her. Mud ran up her legs past her knees, reminding him of old-fashioned stockings. She was holding the gourd. As he left he realized how lovely her shoulders were.

Zules began walking, unsure of direction and not really caring. The night sky had temporarily cleared to a black sheen filled with stars. He could feel the water in his boots, the weight of mud on his back. He shut down his mind and walked, glad for the necessity of motion. From everywhere came the steady sound of dripping water.

A police car slowed in a crossroads and stopped beside him. The deputy was driving. He wasn't wearing his badge or uniform, and Zules felt as if a hellhound had finally found his trail. As the water rose, he was sinking. He was going to be killed and lost in the flood and he didn't really care. He was tired. For his mother's sake, he hoped that someone would find his body. It occurred to him that dying on a cold wet night was no worse than a fine autumn day.

"How's she doing?" the deputy said.

"My mother? They'll knock her in the head on Judgment Day."

"You know who I mean," the deputy said. "Is she all right?"

"Not exactly."

"Get in."

"I'm pretty bad muddy."

"Doesn't matter. It's a county car."

"I don't really need a lift."

"Just get in the stinking car. I'll run you by your motel."

Zules walked around the hood and slid in the front seat and the deputy made a U-turn. He drove past blinking yellow lights on sawhorses that blocked flooded streets. All the houses were dark. People sat on the porches holding flashlights and rifles.

The deputy stopped at the motel. A maple by the door had been hit by lightning and the lot was covered with wood chips and twigs. Zules could smell the fresh scent of the tree's inner meat. The burn mark ran to the ground.

"Charges are dropped," the deputy said.

"That state trooper clear me?"

"No. We got a witness. An old man saw a car leaving the scene. He can put the driver in it, too."

The deputy sighed. He shifted his body toward Zules. His voice was low and sad, defeated.

"I know who did it."

"Anyone else know?" Zules said.

"Not unless you do."

"What about the witness?"

"He's an old river rat," the deputy said. "Long as he don't get busted for running trotlines, he won't say nothing."

"And if he did, nobody'd believe him."

"About like you."

"In that case," Zules said, "I best be leaving."

A shower came over the car, the drops rapid as if a squirrel ran along the roof. The rain moved down the street. The motel's neon sign abruptly went out. Lightning flashed on the horizon and Zules realized that he'd been hearing the dull rumble of thunder for a long time. It was coming from everywhere, like the rain.

He opened the car door but the deputy's voice stopped him. "I don't know what to do. I thought I did but I'm not sure anymore. You ever get that way?"

"That's why I left home."

"I've never lived anywhere but this place."

"How come you to be a cop?"

"Just like to see things run smooth, I guess. I know everybody here, who their folks are and their kids. Every little thing they do. I know who steals and who looks in windows and who sleeps with who. I'm tired of it, too. But the knowing keeps me here."

"Same thing drove me off my hill."

The deputy grinned, a thin expression that was gone fast. "Real reason is, ten years ago I couldn't afford a car. I let the county give me one."

"That's why I took my first driving job."

"But you can move on."

"I'd rather be a stayer."

Zules walked to his truck and climbed into the cab. He let the engine warm up, feeling its power vibrate through his body, relaxing him. He felt safe. It was the highest above ground he'd been since leaving jail. Sheetrock was right about the safety of the cell. Zules decided to give him a call in a few days, same as he would his mother.

Zules opened his map and stared at the red and blue highway lines until they blurred like veins under skin. He was pretty close to the edge of the country, with nowhere to go. He sat in the truck for a long time, looking into the darkness. The wet land was flat as tin. He decided to go to the hills for good. He was thirty-one, with no ex-wife and a little money. There'd be someone to marry him. He could get his own place then. He'd sell the truck and apply for work, maybe as a cop. He thought he'd make a good one.

Rain fell in waves and his headlights were dull against the fog. He put the truck in gear and headed home, moving into second and third carefully. It was dangerous to drive fast without a trailer behind him. He needed a heavy load to keep him stable.

"High Water Everywhere" originally appeared in *Gentleman's Quarterly*, December 1994.

Johanna Stull
Daniel Woodrell

Eugene's partners have gathered on the gravel bar below the rapids at Tulla Bridge, where so many tourists in canoes take spills and lose watches, rings, cameras, sunglasses and so much else, adding their treasure to our riverbed, and Eugene wanted me there. He wants me along as his witness when he tells this bunch how he's not worried about the mailman any more, that testimony won't get said, and the cows can be moved to a sale barn in a few days or a week. Buster Leroy Dolly is sitting on a folding chair, bare feet in the Twin Forks, canned beer between his legs, and a handful of other fully dressed fellas also hang about, smoking weed, snorting stuff that snorts, conspiring idly and drinking plenty in the fine sunshine.

When tourists roll over the rapids the men shout numbers at them, ranking their water skills from one to ten, watching them panic when the canoes take air over the rocks, or slap about uncertainly with their paddles and spill sideways. Nobody on the gravel bar is dressed for the beach but they stand as a chorus near the lip of the river and point, laugh, suggest to the pretty that they could become dear friends right quick, all those things. The tourists glance over, scowl or grin if they don't tip, listen to their scores and paddle faster downstream. They don't seem to mind the scoring much. We are cousins at some remove, me and most of these men, but I never cared for this bunch and they never cared for me back, which leaves us kin and almost strangers.

Eugene is high for the day, the mailman cooled, whiskey bottle passing, that shit he snorts when he wants to feel his head get turned over, emptied of echoes. He gives me a squeeze, a rap on the arm, and says I did okay, have fun, welcome home again and everything. Eugene high is a person I avoid even more. When he shouts numbers, the tourists sense the deep wrongness in him and paddle harder if they don't spill. If they spill they have to scramble and splash to the gravel bar in their cut-off shorts, wet T-shirts, bikinis, and feel his shadow lay over their skin.

"Which college is it you girls go to? Like a hand rightin' your canoe?"

Buster Leroy, the next boss in line, has a quick smile and dimples and no fear of anything breathing, though he is careful with Eugene. He's of the right bloodline for the throne hereabouts, the throne in the shadows, and he waves me to his side. He's wearing khakis hiked up to the knees, and a blue shirt with the tiny crocodile over the heart. His hair is combed upwards and backwards, a blondish swoop with fractures of white running above the ears, ending in a duck tail long enough to knot. Little clouds of fish jerk around his toes nibbling. His smile almost fools you. He says, "Well, now—I see you went off and lived through it, young cuz."

"So they tell me."

"Good on you. Welcome back to the world." He swatted a hand that hit my knee like a pat on the back and raised dust. "I been wonderin' how's your grandma doin'."

"Her heart might quit, but she won't."

"Never believed she would. We used to throw walnuts at each other, little kids, second grade or so.

56

Third." He stared down and out at circles on the water he studied as the river skated south. It was a long broody stare to take among company. Then his head raises. "Reckon that mailman'll be forgetful now?"

"He needs his health."

"That's sure as hell true—mailman like that has got to have his health."

"I won't be ridin' shotgun for any more of that shit."

"Didn't like what you saw, huh?"

"Didn't like seein' it here."

Buster Leroy cranked his head around and his eyelids drew back flattened as he stared at me. The greased style his hair was combed up into was pretty olden, yet many roadhouse gals of today liked his style plenty when his eyelids weren't flattened that way. He made me wait a spell, staring his power into my chest, trying to command my blood to flow backwards, maybe, then said, "You ain't goin' to be partnerin' with Eugene?"

My feet were sinking into the gravel and water gathered over my boots, starting out to drown me slow from the toes on up. I put more weight on my heels to dig down further.

"Not in this lifetime."

A canoe carrying two heavy fellas in armless shirts got hung up on the rocks at the little drop below the bridge. The tip stuck out three feet above the water but the middle had gone aground, and when the fellas grunted, grunted and shoved loose, they went nose down too straight and scattered everything they had into the current. The partners on the gravel laughed, hooted, pointed, but somebody shouted them a rating of ten, anyhow, since they kindly donated so much shiny new shit to us.

Buster Leroy said, "Good— I won't have any big problems with you somewhere down the line then, will I?"

This bunch counts on fear to mold you. Their histories tend to bully you, till your insides and plant numerous fears of them that grow higher in your guts the more you know them. They are bullying you even when they're smiling, slapping your back, saying good to see you again, calling you cuz.

I said, "You never do know. That's what you learn."

The girl had crawled under a low willow above the riverbank and is still hiding from the sky and everybody else when I approach. Flashlights are shining around, a couple at the willow, the others at Eugene, who is shitfaced and mumbly, mostly undressed, lurching along the gravel bar, dark scratches on his chest. The girl is curled up, looking straight down toward something certain and invisible, shivering, showing sunburned shoulders and a pale stripe where her swimsuit strap belonged. I only see her in spots as the lights bounce about. The noise of the rapids is so much louder in the night. Spots of light bouncing sudden pictures.

Somebody says, "We wondered where he'd slunk away to, then we heard screams and knew."

"How come me?"

Buster Leroy says, "He's your fuckin' daddy, that's how come you. This one's a local girl, too, from town, here. Them canoe people'll be lookin' for her by now. You best take care of her, understand? Carry her to a doc or somewhere and tell her how it goes testifyin' against Eugene."

I bent to the girl, spread the curtain of whips and

58

scooted close under the willow. She made a sound I hurt to hear, shivered more. Her nose is risen into a bitter lump, with blood and snot fallen in tangles onto her chin and chest. Her swollen top lip is bloused over the bottom. She's squeezing the panty-piece in her hands, the bra-part of the suit is gone. I get a grip and tug her standing. She's sleepwalking now. She just squeezes those striped bright bottoms.

"Put those on, won't you?"

Somebody says, "I don't believe I ever was even here."

She steps into the leg holes slowly, like she's standing on something brittle that might snap apart and she'd fall through to the lava pit if she stepped down hard, then crosses her arms. I pulled my shirt off and pulled it around her, shook her to get her arms open, hands through the sleeves, buttoned the buttons, and her eyes cringed in their holes and looked through me by then. I held her arm to guide her across the dirt in the dark, over to the truck, and set her inside. There's vomit in her hair. Everybody starts leaving the river where they never saw a thing, never even were, slamming doors, rumbling motors, a quick convoy gunning tires away from this scene. She makes that hurting sound again. I said, "Don't blow." She looks at me all bewildered and bashed, a girl who woke rested in a familiar world and will be sleepless a while in this sudden new one. "Nose. Air might get in there and swell your face up worse."

The headlights cut a short lane in front of the truck. I can't see far but I'm rolling hard. She's clutched up to the door, this hurt town girl, window down, wind pushing the soiled yellow hair from her face. Her legs are bruised with his fingerprints and her toenails are painted blue. She keeps staring at me, bruised good and hoping hard I won't become her next nightmare.

"That man'll get after you and stay after you if you call the law."

It was the shivering of her body that just drew me in, let me know her deep of a sudden, the puffing of her face and the vomit in her hair let me know her more, in that way hurt knows hurt. Her legs stretch to the floor, her hands come down and grab her knees. That hair flutters so yellow and mussed. Then a streak of recall hits her, I get it, I get it, I do know well that quick dumping of wrong feelings or thoughts or memories of fearful instants or ugly deeds that take over the screen and flicker scenes in your head whenever you don't want them, and she raises her hands to her face and goes away behind her palms. She has to breathe through her mouth, each breath like dry limbs rubbing. I feel dizzy just then, too.

She sickens again on a curve and I yank the truck onto the shoulder. Her knees drop to the floorboards and she's chucking the scrapings from her gut in small doses. A puddle is arranged there, not in a circle, but spread thin and bumpy with salad bits. I grabbed a rag from under the seat and swabbed at her, rubbed puke from her hair, blood from her neck, then turned her face to me and wiped the drool, raised her back onto the seat. I felt her breath carry onto me. Not far down the road, I said, "It's a bad man you run into, and he'll come to your house, too, hurt you and yours, do about anything."

Nothing else gets said—sentences shoot away from me and dive into darkness fast as minnows in the mind. It's a dank, clabbering quiet between us all the way to West Table, and I drive her to the town hospital, pull in on the emergency-room side. There's nobody standing there, just glaring overhead lights and a glass double-door. I run around the truck to help her out and she lets me touch her, touch her fingertips. She stands under the bright arch and brigades of bugs beating away against every light above, in my old shirt and her stained white bottoms. Her eyes are on me, wounded tight. There's a nurse in the hallway.

I said, "I hate to see this happening here."

When you scare things you're going to eat, you sour their taste. I tried to herd the cows gently, without making them bawl or bolt, but Eugene and his partners just whacked at them with sticks and hollered, pushing them toward the loading chute. The truck had markings that were too faded to read, and the cows went into the little pen of iron bars and filed right up the ramp as more whacks landed. This day had the windiest weather since I came back and my skin felt called to the mood of the sky, fluttered. I stood off to the side of the chute, part hidden behind the trailer door, but the cows' eyes kept finding me as they went up, giving big grave looks of things that know and know there's no way out and say it to me in those doomed looks that say it all anywhere you go. Several adults shit on the ramp and the calves stretched their necks to the limit and screamed and pissed streams.

Eugene said, "Smells like payday!"

Colors jumped up and splashed in my head as I walked the pasture—various blues, odd whites, those nervous greens so alert they hum in the brain. The sun was sulky in the sky behind early clouds and I walked around the red clay wallow, the pasture empty now, missing the cows that had rambled amidst so much good grass and rested in the shade. When I hopped the north fence all that emptiness watched me go.

Eugene was outside the hay barn, banging away at his truck, a truck I considered white, or close to white, trying to loosen the lugs on a wheel with a gleaming black tire. He said, "About time, Colonel Purple Heart. Plenty of repairs need doin' 'round here—pitch in." Eugene gives me orders so freely. I said, "Aye, aye." Those lugs are not coming loose, and he hunkers low to beat at them with a small hammer, break the crud and rust away. There's a heavy pipe in the junk pile that fits my hand. He's squatted by the gleaming tire, banging that hammer, my rough-cob daddy, and I stepped closer to his bent back, hefted the pipe. One good whack opened his head and dropped him to the dirt, and I stood back to keep my boots clean. He wiggled on the dirt quite a bit and dumped. Running blood kept making me inch backwards.

His stink came and went like a shit ball the wind kicked.

I sat on a stump, stretched my legs and listened to morning birds in the pasture, waiting for his chest to stop pumping, feet to stop shaking. The skull bone had opened enough to see something gummy was contained in there, and the bone was a moistened whiteness inside a shawl of scalp and hair that was slightly flung back from the split. Blood escaped through the split and down his skin but turned to thick gunk in the dust. Busted heads always make a puddle.

My bones had sweetened to the root swinging that pipe.

He still heaved and one foot yet jittered when Grandma stood behind me. She'd come quiet up the pasture and around the fence. She was in hospital slippers and a summery dress with the color washed from it, her homemade sunbonnet, face showing sadness, limbs quivering. I said, "You walked here?"

"I heard you sittin' in my room all night."

"You shouldn't walk that far, Grandma."

"I had a feelin' when you got up so slow and went out the door."

"It's a strain on you."

"I noted you walked off like you had somewhere you needed to go." She bent to her son and listened to the twanging sounds from his interior. "Oh, I reckon Eugene's been aimed at a finish like this all his life." Her legs gave way and she knelt beside him, knees in his blood, and laid a hand on his back. She felt the rise and fall. "You know, he ain't dead yet. He's still breathin'. He's not all the way dead."

"Stand back."

Her eyes would understand me even when she was gone.

"That ain't the way to do. You know that. He's still breathin'—I have to call."

"He did somethin' I hate to see, Grandma. Somethin' terrible again."

"That's how he does. Who he is. Always has been." She pushed up, mud made of Eugene clung to her knees, and came to me, put her arms all around me, talked into my ear. She smelled like so many corners in the cellar. "I'm fixin' to die, Cookie. Go to God. Not far off, neither. And I surely don't want to be carryin' my own son's murder with me while I shake and shake them gates."

"You think them gates are there?"

"I can feel my hands around the bars."

When our hug broke, I looked at Eugene, then said, "I've known worse hurt that lived."

At our house I went inside Eugene's room. It catches you off-guard to see how tidy he kept things there, a habit of order he picked up living six years in a cell. Everything neatly put away in dresser drawers or the little closet. The old wood in that room had been marred by antique dents and browned gouges but he'd sanded it new while still wearing Department of Corrections clothing and polished it just so. The only pictures on the walls are calendars from different years, the kind with tanned women in short-shorts and hard hats showcasing power tools, special saws, hammers that won't miss. Grandma goes for the phone. A small drawer was left part open by his bed, and I slide it on out, look inside. There are three pocket knives in the drawer, the dinky kind for slitting letters open or cutting chaw, a packet of sugar-dipped cigars like drunk kids smoke, and five driver's licenses, all of women, collected from each so he could find them again if charges were filed. I go through with a slow shuffle, looking at faces, taking my time, looking until I see that color hair.

There's a chopper coming down to land in the pasture while I squat on an old rock wall inside the timber line swallowing the facts of this girl, the numbers of her life, and wash from the chopper blades storms the trees and makes limbs panic and leaves jump to ground. It's her face without the damage, and she near about smiles. She's two years older and has gained weight since and let her hair get dangly. The radio on the chopper squawks and bleats and I can't keep from getting to one knee, fixing to run and hop aboard, like the chopper is my unexpected transport into or out of some close by or far off fight I'd been assigned to, couldn't guess who with. My teeth grind and grind and I sit back on rocks and put her face into my shirt pocket. Grandma stands leaning on the north fence, dress tightened against her by the gust, sunbonnet gone, a few scatterings of limp hair to blow, waving the medics toward Eugene.

The doctor says I saved him for now without knowing it was me. "He was hit so hard on the head he's got a chance to live." Doc's from some other country, wearing a white coat, no smile, a necktie part stuffed into a white breast pocket, the pointed ends swaying when he gestures. He says the way I cracked the bone open took pressure off Eugene's brain by letting the blood gutter away to reduce swelling. Doc's voice ranges high at odd words in his sentences, gives him a strange beat it takes a minute to catch on to, then he's a song from overseas, basically. "Sorry to say he won't be the same again, but we might one day be able to return the man to his home."

Grandma says, "He'll live to go home?"

"Or, he could pass tonight, brains being so very difficult to predict."

Me and her take seats in the ICU waiting room. There are glossy magazines stacked around, most all of them dedicated to subjects I couldn't care about, so I thumbed through a dozen, glancing at the ads, mostly, plus recipes for meals I didn't understand. I have one opened on my lap, and I'm using a licked thumb to grip the pages as I toss through them, and Grandma reaches over and pushes the magazine shut.

She says, "You better act like you care. You better act like you care somebody bashed Eugene in the head."

"I'll care most if he lives."

"You'll care right quick if Buster Leroy'n them others guess it was you."

Do civilian hospitals make the hallways extremely

glowing on the floors and pearly on the walls so the doped and dying might see the shimmering around them as they are wheeled here and there and think they are already inside the shine of heaven? Maybe people don't hurt as much inside the shining. I had been in a dulled one that was dirty, plain old dirty and crowded, with vague, drifting nurses and men without all their parts or minds moaning from grayish beds in gray light for their meds, meds for pain or fear that were always late in coming, and the doctors would shuffle through once in a while without making eye-contact but writing patient evaluations on a clipboard. There were cracks in the forgotten walls and broken windows and broken sounds. Screams and quiet, screams and quiet, and in the quiet moments loping echoes of the screams kept roaming your head. Soon you started claiming to the staff you were well way before you were, learned what answers a well person would give and gave them, over and over, just to leave the ward and the stink of oozed blood from yesterday. I guess it smelled like payday in there for somebody behind a desk in the distance who wouldn't ever feel anything but the money.

She has that loneliness light inside her house; shades pulled, lamps not turned on, just a smear of sunshine through the window above the kitchen sink. You can see the lonesome facts in different rooms if you stand and bend your neck to look; the one dinner plate, the one tea cup in the sink with a teabag string looped around the handle, the dog bowl full of spare change on the dresser next to a worn dog collar, the skinny bed against the wall, fuzzy childish slippers underneath. She listens to the radio station that announces everything for sale by owner, one voice after another calling in to get shed of that old fridge with the loud motor, the backhoe that smokes, a three-piece couch, two spools of cable, the last goat and a rubber canoe that has never been floated. Most of the voices are calm, but others really need to make a sale and the needy pitch of their words lets you know you could bid them awful low and carry their stuff away.

She said, "This saves me a trip to the DMV—am I supposed to thank you?"

Her face is in the ugly stage of healing, blended bruises making colors no single word fits, but the swelling around her eyes is down. I was surprised she let me inside at all. "Plus, he's in the hospital with a caved-in head."

"Will he die?"

"There's a real good chance of it. Doctor said that." She seemed alert to me but not quite scared, and wore a white skirt, ninety-nine cent flip-flops, a green T-shirt. Her yellow hair hung lank and straight, maybe needed a wash. It was still daylight, and in daylight she might be willing to go see him. "Let me show you how the man is now. It could mean something to you."

She had her answer ready.

"I'll follow in my own car, take one look."

"Meet in the front lobby."

In the lobby she said, "I don't know about this."

"There's no way this'll make anything worse."

"There's always a way."

Inside that shine we walk down different hallways to the ICU waiting room, her trailing me but not by much. Buster Leroy and three others are sitting around with a side-table pulled up close to their knees, playing poker. There are stacks of dollars in the pot and stacks before each man, and an unhappy nurse with a hand on her hip is standing there. Buster Leroy says, "We ran out of matchsticks, darlin', so we had to switch to money to keep score with."

"We can't have gamblin' goin' on in here, Mr. Dolly."

"We're not gambling. Gambling is done for money. We're only playing for matchsticks."

Inside the ICU a male nurse hops up as the double-doors close behind us, and asks, "Are you family?"

"You saw me here all night, didn't you? This is his daughter, come from somewhere else."

The curtain around Eugene is a wasted-away greenish color. I just pulled it around on the circular rods. He is covered to his neck. His head is tilted way back with a big gadget hooked to the bed frame that clamps at his temples and neck to hold it still. There's a sort of cheesecloth spread over the spot where I bashed him. His head has fattened. Tubes run here and there, and there's a wheezing machine. The room is very much brightened by the late sun.

She stares at Eugene and her own skin pales. Her feet move side-to-side.

"You can do whatever you want to him," I whisper. "I'll watch the door."

"I couldn't do a thing to him."

"Would it make you feel good to at least smack him?"

"I wouldn't feel right about that."

"You hadn't ought to do it, then, if you already know you wouldn't feel right."

She turns to me in all that brightness, looks up with that healing face and asks, "Did you do this?"

But footsteps come up behind me while I'm pondering, a hand squeezes my shoulder. I smell his hair oil as he squeezes.

"I need to borrow him for a minute," Buster Leroy

says to her. He's pulling me along and his grip sort of hurts. "Come on, cuz, walk with me."

She's gone when we come back, so I head the truck her way. He'd wanted to tell me I could turn to him if I ever needed to talk. He knew by my face at the river I wasn't home yet. We could rap, dredge it up, get it all out. He mentioned Eugene only once, said he knew who bashed him, but didn't want me to say so. There was no need. It's over and done. The sun is pretty gone down and there are trees in the way, but it's not dark, just softened. There's an ice cream truck on the road making music that calls kids. He said there's no point in talking to civilians, Cookie, 'cause you could talk for a week and a day and they'd never get it. People who don't know shit like to say to your face they would never have done what you did, man, not to anybody, or would've done it better, or their goody-goodness wouldn't allow them to be in such circumstances as you had been in, ever, or even look at the pictures. If they haven't seen guts on the ground, brother, it's just too frustrating to talk with them. They can't hear you. Some of them only want to see you cry. I note that she has closed the blinds and the lights are off.

She's hiding.

I hop up the porch steps and knock. The door opens barely a crack. I can see it's open, but can't see anything inside there. She says, "You need to go away."

"I could help out, mow your lawn—getting shaggy by the curb, there."

"No. Go away. Anytime I see his face, your face is right beside his. I see his face, I see your face, and I don't want to see either. You make me see both."

The door shuts on me and I turn to face the street.

Buster Leroy had told a story about how he'd been a Forward Observer with two other guys and had gotten cut off in the jungle when a regiment that wasn't supposed to be there appeared of a sudden and went rushing past to attack the base on every path and through the trees. Buster Leroy and his guys had to crawl into a tiny hole. The hole went straight down. They had to crawl in one at a time. They spent five days stacked in that hole hoping they weren't seen or smelled and our own bombs wouldn't get them by mistake. The bottom guy in the hole went nuts on day three, which is better than it sounds.

"Johanna Stull" appeared in the *Buffalo Almanack*.

Where Cat Scratch and Happy Valley Meet
Patrick Michael Finn

The first time I clocked the plan to rip off Happy Valley Liquor, I was stuck at the back of the goddamn line with a six-pack of Mickey's Big Mouths, moving my weight from one leg to the other to stop the throbbing hurt up inside my feet from standing at the taco grill all day.

Every night I stood there waiting with all the twisted fuckheads from around Cat Scratch. Drunks, rotting meth-mouths, dirtbag old whores. Lot of vagrants roaming through. Indians, wetbacks, insane freight train hoppers with beef jerky skin and names like Lester and Cheeks.

A while back, there was a family in Cat Scratch who lived in a station wagon. Mom, Dad, two little daughters, and a baby. They had all their shit packed up in that car and they hardly had room to move. Sometimes they got a motel. I saw them buying food at Happy Valley Liquor—crackers, hotdogs, cans of beans, baloney. One time when this family stayed in the motel over in Colton, the father found a rat in the bathroom cabinet under the sink and decided to trap it and keep it for a pet. Then they were back in the station wagon, but the father still had the rat in a shoebox and fed it crackers from his fingers. His wife wouldn't touch it and told him to get rid of it. But the children were happy and clapping, and the baby giggled whenever he took it out of the shoebox. When the rat snapped at her husband and took a chunk out of his knuckle, the wife screamed at him to get that damned rat out. He told her it was all right and put the rat away. One night when everyone was asleep, the rat chewed its way out, crawled up to the baby in his car seat, sleeping with a cracker, and that rat bit and gnawed the baby to death. That's the kind of place this was, and just living there alone was enough to make you sick and mean. In the middle of it all was Happy Valley Liquor. And that goddamn line killed my legs so bad after standing at the grill all day that my balls hurt. There was always only one woman, a big older lady who didn't mind taking her time, working behind the counter.

My head cleared and got cool and I saw and figured it out. One fat lady working the counter for a whole hour. One fat lady working with a line that wouldn't quit being long. The stock room was way down on the other side of the counter from where the register was. The stock room door was only cracked, and inside it was dark.

I went out like I was walking back to the bus stop and then I made a long walk around to the back of the liquor store, where there was an alley and a big fence for the San Bernardino switchyards. I found the stock room door and it was unlocked. I opened it and didn't even look inside.

The only problem was I didn't have a car, so the next night after work I called Filthy Phil Rick. I told him to pick me up and we'd go over to the cocktail lounge at the Thunderbird Lanes and have a drink. I had to explain things to him slowly, because he's kind of half retarded. I'm not sure how he got his license, but he had one. I made him show me.

"Oh?" he said. "Here in my billfold, Wayne."

It was his picture. His puffy face and those big stupid glasses. He was on disability for bipolar disorder and lived with his mother. When I told him his share and what we'd be taking, he got excited. I had to tell him to quiet the hell down. I could have punched him.

I wanted to get out of my job, bad. I had to do it for the San Bernardino County Welfare to Work plan. July and August it got up to a hundred and twenty in that truck. And Rudy, the owner, my boss, always had the noisy radio on the Mexican station. Accordion, horns, little greasers whining. Rudy was all right though. I've worked for some straight-up cocksuckers, but Rudy never gave me any shit. He worked just as hard as me in that oven.

The only soap we had to wash with in the sink was dish soap. I had to wash my hands after I went out for a cigarette or took a leak, so I had to wash my hands a lot. Rudy'd gotten the dish soap at a cheap Mexican store, and that soap was raw. My hands got real white and dry. If I made a fist, a scab would crack and bleed. One morning I was wrapping up a chorizo and egg burrito for this Mexican dude. He was watching me do it, saw my ugly sores and walked away without his order.

"Hey, man!" I said, but he just put his hands in his pockets and left. He'd already paid, so there was nothing I could do, and he didn't ask for his money back. He didn't get his drink either, orange Jarritos. Still, I felt ashamed.

I qualified for free groceries from the San Bernardino Transitional Authority Food Bank. They sent a couple bags once a week, but I hated the shit that was in them. Spam, cheese, noodles, chicken broth, canned stew tomatoes. I usually ended up throwing most of it away. They even included a little recipe pamphlet with a picture on it of a happy black family cooking in the kitchen. I laughed at that. I didn't want their goddamn food. I mostly ate at work.

I hit Happy Valley Liquor for the first time on a Wednesday night, a Super Lotto night. I told Filthy Phil, "Just drive like you're going home from getting Burger King." I propped the stockroom door with a cinderblock and told Filthy Phil to stand by the car and watch. I moved about ten boxes. Then I got a box packed with cartons of cigarettes.

I lived where Cat Scratch and Happy Valley meet, up in a room in a big complex subsidized by San Bernardino County called Palm Vistas. I had Filthy Phil pull the Buick around and park behind the basketball courts where there were lights because I wanted to open the trunk and take a look at what I'd gotten.

"Holy shit," I said. "Seagrams, Early Times, Jim Beam, Kentucky Tavern, Cutty Sark, Bacardi." I moved some of the boxes out onto the pavement. "Heaven Hill, Gordon's, Captain Morgan, Cruzan, Juarez Gold, Presidente, Pepe Lopez, and Rio Grande."

There were twenty cartons of cigarettes, only they were bottom-shelf brands like L&M's, Raleighs, Viceroys, Dorals, Magnums, Larks, Old Golds, and Kents. I thought I could probably move them. Hell, I'd smoke them if I had to. I opened a carton of Old Golds and stuck two packs in my pocket.

"Hey, let me have some cigarettes!" Filthy Phil said. The way he said it sounded like "sea-grits." He was born in Oklahoma, and even though he'd been in California nearly all his life, sometimes he still talked like a hick. I tossed him a pack.

We hauled all the boxes up to my room.

"Let's have a drink!" he said.

"Only one," I told him.

But we ended up getting trashed on a bottle of Early Times. I blacked out and woke up sick and late for work and Phil was passed out on the floor with a black eye and there was puke all over my hot plate and dripping down some of the boxes. The room stank like hell. I woke Phil up and he cowered when he saw me.

"What the hell's the matter?" I asked.

"You punched me out!" he said. It was when he'd thrown up, he told me. I knocked him around and then I wouldn't let him leave. He was too drunk to drive and I didn't want him to get busted because I needed his Buick.

"Sorry," I said. "I was drunk."

Rudy was pissed that I was late to work, but I'd never been late before, so he didn't fire me. I wouldn't have cared if he did. I pretty much figured I wasn't going to be there much longer.

Because when I got off work Friday night, I had Filthy Phil pick me up. It was still early. The sun was hot and red in our faces when we parked around behind Palm Vistas and opened the trunk. A pair of Mexican dudes splattered with white paint walked by. I'd seen them get off the bus.

"Hey, amigos," I said. "Check this out, hombres."

The Mexican guys liked what we had and they bought two bottles of Gordon's vodka and two packs of Raleighs. Then a few minutes later a leathery dude in a Raiders cap came by and bought a bottle of Cruzan. Men coming out of the building just to get some shit out of their cars walked by and bought bottles of Gordon's, Bacardi, Seagrams, Beam, Captain Morgan, Rio Grande. Pretty soon we had a line. I put Filthy Phil to work. I took the cash and yelled orders over my shoulder and he dug around in the trunk.

Hours went by and parties were raging all up and down the building. By two, the trunk was nothing but a bunch of empty boxes, not one bottle or single smoke left besides the half-empty pack of Old Golds in my pocket. I'd made three thousand bucks in nine hours.

Back up in my room, I gave Filthy Phil five hundred. He thought that was some kind of jackpot, and he punched the air with his fist and barked. I couldn't blame him. I actually laughed.

"Come on, let's go get a drink," he growled. Jesus, Filthy Phil Rick sure was a piece of work. He could sit there like a chunk of dogshit and not say a word for eight hours straight, then something would get him wild and he'd jabber you into next month. Sometimes I'd get so sick of listening to all his bullshit that I'd start feeling like I was bipolar in my own head, and I'd sit there grinding my teeth and think about cutting his head off with a shovel. I didn't like feeling so mean. It burned in my brain with anger, anger, anger. I'd tell Filthy Phil to get the fuck out and I'd crash and lay there on my bed feeling like a piece of garbage.

"All right," I said. "Let's roll."

But when we got downstairs, we realized it was almost three. All the bars were closed and none of the gas stations sold beer after two. Both of us sort of sank.

"Aw, goddamnit," Filthy Phil said. "Goddamnit just all to hell," he said, and sagged forward and let his arms hang.

* * *

I slept late and got up Saturday afternoon. I was glad I hadn't gotten trashed the night before. I wanted to enjoy my money, and I did. I went and got a haircut and a shave.

I told the barber, "Put some of that extra bay rum on my neck!"

"Yes, sir," he said. I tipped him five bucks and went out and waited at the bus stop, smoking a cigarette. I'd never had so much cash in my whole goddamn life, and while I wasn't stupid with the money, I'd been broke long enough and for once I finally had a chance to stretch out and live.

I took the bus to the Fontana Swap Meet at the Skylight drive-in and bought a few new pairs of Wrangler jeans and some Wrangler shirts with pearly metal snaps. Then I blew a hundred on some pointed Mexican snakeskin boots. I got a Boker gravity knife with horn handles, the kind you just flip your wrist and the stiletto blade flashes out and locks in place. I saw it shining there on a display table and said, I've got to have that motherfucker.

Saturday night I looked good over at the Thunderbird Lanes cocktail lounge, knocking back the Jack and Cokes. I sat at my own table so I could get served, and I played George Jones on the jukebox and kicked back with my feet up so the waitresses could see my new boots.

I expected the stockroom to be double-locked with new bolts the next Wednesday night when Filthy Phil and I hit Happy Valley Liquor. But it was open again and loaded with twice as much booze. I packed the Buick's trunk and the backseat with twenty cases of liquor and forty cartons of smokes, and that weekend we worked the lot behind the Palm Vistas both Friday and Saturday night until damn near four in the morning. I made six grand, and I gave Filthy Phil seven hundred along with a carton of Larks and two bottles of Kentucky Tavern. "Shitting pissfire," he hissed.

Then Sunday night I was back at the Thunderbird Lanes buying rounds for whole league teams of strangers who shook my hand and offered me smokes. I called a black guy I knew from Happy Valley, Stylish Price. He drove over and sold me an eight ball in the parking lot. Then I took two of the lane waitresses over to a motel and snorted blow and drank tequila with them all night and fucked the pink off of them both.

I was still wired and drunk when I went into work Monday afternoon to tell Rudy I was through. "Where the hell you been?" he yelled over the counter. I'd never seen him that furious. There was a line of five and he was alone. "Get your ass in here!"

"Oh, man," I said. "I'm sorry, Rudy. You've been a good boss and all, but I'm quitting now."

He smashed the door open and ran out and got in my face right there on the sidewalk. "You're supposed to give two weeks," he said, and shoved me. "You're supposed to give two weeks' notice," he said, and shoved me again. The guys in line spread out, staring, and I put up my hands and tried to tell Rudy to back off. I just wanted to leave, but he kept pushing me, pushing me. I don't know if it was because I was sort of messed up and geeked out or what, but a flash lit up behind my eyes and I grabbed a fistful of Rudy's apron and lifted him so fast that his face turned white and his mouth got wide and he sucked in wind like a kid on a carnival ride. I marched him across the sidewalk and pounded his whole body against the side of the truck, again and again and again. It sounded like someone slamming a sledgehammer against an empty Dumpster, and the truck jolted in place with each pound. Then I dropped him on the curb and he landed on his side by the tire. I was surprised I didn't knock him out. When I looked back about a half block away, the dudes who'd been waiting in line were helping Rudy up, holding his arms, and he was touching the back of his head.

Filthy Phil and I stole liquor and cigarettes for weeks. We started working the parking lot on Thursdays, even Sunday afternoons. It was late August and we were both always wired and trashed. And Cat Scratch was just as fucked up as we were. A lady upstairs passed out from the liquor we sold her. She had a cigarette going, and her bed caught fire. She burned to death and two other apartments got completely gutted.

Another night, a drunk husband threw his pregnant wife out the window ten flights down, broken glass and all, and her spine cracked. She died and so did the baby. Someone found a dead whore in a Dumpster behind the Grocery Outlet. She'd been slashed across the tits, gagged, strangled, and she had a broken broomstick shoved up her ass.

I know I shouldn't have let Filthy Phil booze and snort as much as he did. It made him more bugged-out nuts than I'd ever seen him. His eyes were red and wild behind his big stupid glasses. Some days I'd see him running down Foothill in the hundred-degree heat, smiling big, completely soaked with sweat. He'd shake and run and the sweat would spray all over. But other times he'd just move down the street with his arms folded over his head, moaning.

He'd wandered away somewhere the afternoon I get beat up and robbed. It was one of those days at the end of August when the smog is so thick you can't see the mountains or the sun, and the world looks like it's sitting on the edge of smoke and fire. I was mostly blacked out, and these two little lowriders clocked me upside the head and got away with about five cases of booze, the last of what I had in the trunk. They took a few hundred bucks off me, too. I got up when they left and staggered around and bumped the empty Buick, yelling about how I was going to skin them. Two San Bernardino Counties pulled up, and I guess I was lucky I'd gotten ripped off. They busted me for public intoxication, and that's all they could get me for. Still, I was kicking the windows and seats in the cruiser all the way to the station, and when we got there, the cops whacked the shit out of me with lead-loaded flat leather saps.

I got out the next night and stayed in bed for about a week. I didn't answer the door when Filthy Phil knocked. He came by two, three times a day. He'd stand in the hallway and yell, "Hey, Wayne! Where the fuck are you, man? I got to talk to you!"

He caught up with me at the Thunderbird Lanes cocktail lounge. Right in front of everybody, he pushed right on up to me and said, "You and me need to talk." He said, "You and me need to talk about M-O-N-E-E, sir. M-O-N-E-E."

I pulled him over to a space in the dark next to the jukebox and said, "You better keep your goddamn mouth shut, Phil. You're going to get our dicks busted right into Chino." I hadn't let go of his arm. "I could've used your help the other day when I got the shit kicked out of me, but I haven't come looking for you."

"M-O-N-E-E," he said.

So I eased up and got him a drink, a beer, and I said, "All right, Phil. What do you and I have to talk about, man?"

"I need more money," he said. "I need more money right now."

"I figured as much, but I have to ask you what you need the money for."

"Oh, I can't tell you," he said.

"You have to."

"My mother kicked me out of the house," he groaned. "I'm living in my car, and I've gotta help Cheyenne."

"Who in the hell's Cheyenne?"

"My girlfriend."

"What goddamn girlfriend?"

She was a stripper, of course. She wasn't anybody's girlfriend, but she knew how to gouge a lonely idiot like Filthy Phil out of everything he had by shaking her tits in his face and smiling whenever he held up a twenty. "And she needs more money so she can get her own place."

"Does she know about the money?"

"Yes, that's how she knew I could get more."

"Aw, Phil, goddamnit."

I told him to come by the next afternoon, but I knew I wasn't going to give that sonofabitch a dime.

I thought it was Filthy Phil banging away on the door the next morning at about eleven-thirty. I'd been up wired all night and I'd decided to just hit him over the head with a pair of batteries I'd tied into a sock and take his Buick down to Mexico with the last three thousand I had left.

But it wasn't Filthy Phil standing in the hallway

when I opened the door. It was one of the two waitresses from the Thunderbird Lanes I'd nailed. She was a lot bigger than I remembered.

"What do you want?" I asked.

"You knocked me up," she said. "And you better be ready to pay when the baby comes."

"Aw, bullshit," I said. "How you even know it's mine?"

She had a doctor's form she pulled out of her purse and she stood there in the hallway waving it around and yelling at me about how she already had three kids, but one of the fathers was locked up in Ironwood, the second one was dead, and the third had been deported back to Mexico.

"And I don't get no child support and now you're gonna pay up, else I'm gonna get the cops up your ass so bad you're gonna shit blood."

"All right, quiet down, come in," I said. She wouldn't budge. "I don't have the money right now."

"Bullshit! You blow hundreds at the Thunderbird bar every night. You're gonna pay up," she said.

There was no use trying to talk to her. She wasn't after the money really. She wanted to be right, to win for once. And she wanted to hang being right and winning on a man, any man. Men had fucked her over her whole life, and she was ready to fuck one of them back. Her hollering was echoing all the way up and down the hallway so that a baby started screaming and people were opening their doors.

"Well hell, look," I said. "I don't know if that baby's mine or not, and you probably fuck fifteen different guys a week."

She jumped at me with her nails and clawed a gash right under my eye, and we both fell inside and somehow the door got kicked shut. At first I just tried to hold her hands off by squeezing her wrists and pulling her to the floor, but she was big and wild and she wanted to scrape my face off, and she was kicking, and so the only thing I could do was grab her head and slam it onto the concrete floor until I heard her skull crack and blood squirted out of her eyes.

When Filthy Phil came by a couple hours later, I pulled out a wad of singles. His face lit up and he stuck the wad in his pants after looking at it a second in his big, soft hand. I'd decided I needed his help.

The dead waitress's body was in the bathroom on some garbage bags. But that's not what I said. I said, "Listen, Phil. You and me might need to head down to Mexico for a while."

I could tell he was already upset.

"It's all right, Phil."

He didn't react one way or another to the dead woman on my bathroom floor. He stood there and looked at her and nodded. "She dead?"

"Yeah, she's dead."

"Don't she work at the Thunderbird Lanes?"

"Yes."

"We taking her to Mexico?"

About thirty miles out of Cat Scratch, on Interstate 15 just south of Corona, Filthy Phil started sweating at the wheel. He winced and kept squinting into the rearview. Then he pressed the gas until we were doing about ninety. I heard the body bump in the trunk. We'd wrapped her in the sheet Filthy Phil had been using since he'd been sleeping in his car.

"Hey, slow it down," I said.

"Wayne, I've got to go home."

"Slow down, Phil."

"I've got to go home now. Cheyenne's waiting."

He pulled off onto the shoulder and stopped.

"You can't turn around here," I told him.

"I have to get home," he growled.

"If I get caught, then you sure as hell get caught, too. And you're looking at some long, hard prison time. You want all them buck faggots making you suck them off?"

He got out of the car because he'd started to cry, and he leaned against the hood with his arms folded over his head. I got out and tried to talk him back inside. I had to chase him off the road, down a ditch, then behind a cluster of boulders and brush that hid us from the roadway.

I grabbed his shirt and he stumbled. "Let's get back in the car, Phil."

The dumb fucker tried to push past me, and the only reason I flipped the gravity knife was to scare him. I held it and slashed at the air in between us, and when I slashed it again, he lurched forward, straight at me, and I ended up plunging that blade right into his neck. The blood sprayed me in the face.

He didn't die right away. He was still spurting when I crushed his skull with the rock.

Maybe you don't ever spend time in places like Cat Scratch or Happy Valley. If you're lucky, you don't have any reason to. You'd hardly believe it was America. In a lot of ways, it isn't. There's no freedom for a stretch of half-retarded drug addicts who don't have the sense it takes to think about the future. The future is only the sunset, and all the twisted fuckheads from around Cat Scratch stumble around toward the sunset until their skin looks like it's been burned by acid. Then they turn into street animals and tear each other up with broken wine bottles. I've been doing a lot of thinking about all that, how it's no surprise where I ended up.

They have me on all sorts of medications and I'm usually pretty clear-headed and a little tired. Two lawyers, young gals from UC Berkeley, came by to tell me how much they wanted to help me get off death row.

"You want to help get me off?" I asked. "One of you can lick my asshole while the other sucks on my balls." I laughed and they left and never came back.

I have to see a behavioral health specialist every week. It seems like a big waste of time, seeing as how they're going to inject me dead in two years. 2010. I'll be like the number of the year. Twenty minus ten is ten, and ten minus ten is zero, which is what I will be.

The doctor asked me if I believed in God.

"Do you?" I asked.

"Yes," he nodded, "I believe that I do."

"Well that's about the dumbest thing I've heard in my whole life," I told him. I crossed my arms and leaned back and shook my head and laughed. "You're an educated man. An expert. And you really think there's a God who gives a hot shot of piss whether you're hurting or happy?" I had to laugh and shake my head again. "If there was a God," I said, "he'd march on down here and fuck us all and cut us up and set us on fire."

"Where Cat Scratch and Happy Valley Meet" first appeared in *Thuglit* issue #37.

Smelt
Joseph D. Haske

In mid-April the bank that leads up to the mouth of the Carp River is a five-mile stretch of shantytown. Whiskey and beer bottles everywhere, the Carp curves and cuts its way through pine, sand, and birch into Lake Huron. Bonfires and frosted taillights mark the way down the dusty path over mud ruts and maple roots. Old men sit smoking on rusted-out tailgates, bologna sandwiches in the cooler, booze at the ready. Kids slosh through sand and clay in pint-sized hip-waders that stretch to their necks. The dippers' nets shine in our headlights when the trail curves the truck toward the water. Dad steers down the campsite road that shadows the river and Uncle Tony tokes up from the passenger side.

"Boys hungry?" Dad tosses back a greasy paper bag with venison and butter sandwiches.

Me, Johnny, Tommy, and Cousin Ryan ride back in the Ford's wood truck bed. Dad rigged the wood frame up and bolted it in when the metal one rusted out. It's painted blue to match the cab, but you can tell it's not a pro job.

Johnny peels most of the napkin from his sandwich. "My bread's all wet," he says.

I take a bite and get a mouthful of napkin. Don't say a word, just spit it out.

"You boys wouldn't make it in the Army," Dad says. He stops for a second to sip his Old Milwaukee. "You don't even imagine some of the shit we ate there, right, Tony?"

Dad slides the rear glass window open all the way and holds out his hand. Styx plays on the eight-track. The smoky mist drifts up through the night pines. Ryan coughs. I'm sitting on the cooler so I slide back, pop the lid, and pass a couple Old Milwaukees in to Uncle Tony and Dad.

"What's the worst thing you ate?" I ask him.

"Bugs, rats, piss," says Uncle Tony. "Hell, your old man even ate a shit sandwich one time, right, Gene?"

"We ate shit sandwiches every day back in the bush." Dad's eyes shift back and forth from the road to the rearview mirror.

Tony looks like the devil with the red glow from the cab around his slick, black hair. Smoke circles hang over his bulletproof cheeks and handle-bar moustache. They must've been talking about Grandpa again, 'cause they got that dead quiet look. Then Tony says, "Pass up a couple three more. Gonna two-fist it." It's more than five months now since Grandpa disappeared, but none of us can forget what happened. Dad says he and Uncle Jack got a plan. Says they'll bring in Uncle Tony. Dad and Tony got more spare time now. Both of 'em laid off from the boats. Old Lester Cronin's gonna get his payback. Dad and Tony were Rangers in the Army.

Dad and Tony don't know it, but I heard Uncle Jack, Dad's baby brother, tell Colonel Henry the Pete Girard story last night. When Dad first came back from Vietnam, he found out his sister, Aunt Karen, got pregnant. Grandma told Dad it was a rape but not to tell Grandpa. The family was waiting for Dad to get home to help take care of Pete. That's when Tony first came up from Texas. Karen kept crying until Dad got the truth out of her. Peter Girard got drunk and forced her. Choked her pretty little neck with his left hand while he fucked her mean. Karen didn't want Dad to hurt Pete 'cause he was her boyfriend right up to the day before, until she found out about Pete's wife in Columbus. Dad told Aunt Karen none of that mattered once Pete did what he did. Pete Girard didn't know Dad or Tony from any other locals. His family always came up in the summer from Ohio since he was a kid, but the only Metzger he knew was Aunt Karen. Jack told Henry it was easy for Dad and Tony to get Pete out to the Carp to dip smelt. They smoked a few joints with Pete behind Cronin's Hardware and sealed the deal. Jack rode out to the river with him, in the back of Tony's Dodge. Says Pete was a cocky drunk—bragged the whole trip out that he didn't have to work 'cause he lived off his old man's money—tire business down in Ohio. He told Jack he was gonna trip acid when he got out to the Carp. Make it all psycho-delic. Pete wasn't much for fishing.

Neither Jack or Pete saw it coming. Jack went to sleep around midnight, and he woke up to the scream. Saw Tony toss something red into a five gallon bucket of smelt. Dad was on top of Pete, holding his right arm down, knee in the small of Pete's back. Tony was holding a bloody buck knife and kicking clumps of ground and dust into Pete's face. Jack heard Dad say, "Guess what's next?" Jack walked over to Tony, asked him what was going on. Saw Pete's hand in the bucket. Dad told Jack, "Go for a walk, you ain't seen nothing. Empty that bucket of smelt while you're at it. It ain't no good no more." Jack dumped the bucket. Then he heard another splash come from behind him. Nobody saw Pete Girard around town after that. Nobody around here missed him.

When Jack got done telling Colonel Henry the story about Pete Girard, he was choked up, but Henry's face didn't change the whole time. All Henry did was puff his cigar and say, "Those're the stains of kin. Yessir—the binding stains of kin." Then Jack looked at me and told me to never tell anybody that story or he'd kill me.

The metallic blue Chevy in front of us pulls off to the left. Dad hits a rut and knocks the sandwich out of little Tommy's hand.

"What's it like to smoke them gooks?" Johnny asks.

"I hope you never find out, boy," says Uncle Tony. Dad looks kind of sober all the sudden. He doesn't say anything, but he's thinking hard.

"What was it like?" I ask him. "Vietnam."

"Different than you think," says Uncle Tony. "This one time we's walking through the jungle. Middle of fucking nowhere, and we hear this noise. Sounds like a baby, but there's nobody 'round, and we're humping through some hot terrain. We're thinking it's a goat but it's a real human fucking baby. Laying there in the paddy, by some plants—look like little palm trees. Sometimes, over there, you might think you're in Florida or Hawaii or some damned place but for the bullets all 'round."

"A baby?" Ryan laughs.

"Sounds like bullshit to me," says Johnny.

"You wanna hear the story or not?" says Tony. "Platoon Sergeant says to leave it, keep going. Lieutenant Boyle says, 'Don't touch it. Might be a booby trap.' What kind of shit is that? Strapping grenades to babies. But these V.C. don't fuck around. Do whatever it takes. We saw the kind of crazy nobody believe—less you were there."

Tony cracks another Old Milwaukee.

There's nowhere good left to park at the river mouth so Dad circles around back to the north side road, over where the sand bar splits the river. When he finds a spot, we all hop out where the tailgate should be while the Ford jumps and sputters dead, headlights aimed at the river bank. Johnny and I run over to the hard, sandy ledge, trying to get a look at the river. It's six feet down—can't see much. The water, coffee and milk color, runs fast till it empties in St. Martin's Bay. The headlights and spotlights all around make it hard to see anything but the steel mesh and poles of the smelt nets. The current crackles loud over old men's bullshit and the C.C.R. that whines through AM radio. The wind rips through hard every few minutes, then calms. I snatch the net away from my little brother Tommy, walk the trail down to the water and start to dip. Can't tell if Tommy's gonna cry or he's just shivering up there in his blue hood. Green and yellow snot leaks from both sides of his red nose. Everything smells like fish, cedar, and smoke. I breathe it all in and step into the muck. The Carp's flow pulls me closer, almost takes me in. Dad anchors me. Must've followed me down. He pulls the collar of my ripped blue coat. Steadies me on the bank.

"This ain't too far from where that kid drowned last year, eh, Gene?" says Uncle Tony from the trail. "Never found him till the next morning. One of the LeVasseur boys. Cory?"

"No, Cody," I say. "Ronnie's little brother."

"Cody. We was here when it happened, eh, Gene? Took least a good six-pack afore his old man figured out he was missing. Suppose you kinda expect it with a family like that. Breed too much. So many little bastards running round there's no 'countability for 'em. Old man never heard of propalactics or what? So drunk he couldn't hardly walk, too. Wasn't long, though, one of them boys was looking to take back the net from that little Cody or Cory. Old LeVasseur 'bout shit himself when he seen the boy gone. Ended that party real quick."

"Had us all out here, shining the river with every light west of Drummond Island," Dad says. "About four in the morning, old man Jacques was down on his knees, crying to God in French. Was daylight by the time that Williams boy saw the red sweatshirt hung up on a root downriver, right that way."

"Half the town needed a jump start that morning," Tony says. "I was one of 'em. So caught up looking for the kid, my headlights was on all night. When the trooper come by, I told him I was good. You know me—I ain't getting help from no fucking pig. Had a quarter pound in my trunk. Almost got stuck out here cause of it—sweating it out till all the porkbellies split. Funny thing, it was LeVasseur himself who give me a jump. A rough shape that poor bastard was in."

"Did you see him, Uncle Tony?" Johnny asks him.

"See who? The LeVasseur boy. Yep, we saw the body. Kid was bloated good, only a few hours in the river, right Gene?"

Dad nods. He's helping Tommy and Ryan dip with the other net. Looks like they're really catching 'em, too. Dad shines the flashlight on the five-gallon bucket to show us. It's filling fast.

"You never told us what happened with the baby," Tommy says.

"The grenade," says Ryan.

"So I see it there. Muddy blanket stuck in a pile of jungle shit. Baby looked clean. Best I could tell, there's no wire. Big stupid bastard I am, I kneel down to it and tell the platoon to clear out. Sergeant Preston says, 'Step away from the baby.' Tells me, 'That's an order, Vega.' He's scared shitless, knows I won't listen to him, and he backs off with the rest of 'em, except your old man. Gene's down on the ground there with me, looking for wires under the baby. I remember we looked at each other, thinking we might be blowed to shit any second. Then I picked it up. Nothing—just stopped crying."

Tony stares out to the dark side of the trail, into the maples. "Then what happened?" I ask. "Did he die?"

"Who?" says Tony.

"In the Nam," I say.

"It was a girl," he says. "About then I got really scared. Started thinking what we was gonna do with it. Couldn't just leave it there. Boyle wanted to, but he was too churchy to order us not to take it. 'I ain't responsible for that damned thing,' he said. 'You wanna get your dick shot off for a little dink baby, that's your business. Dumbass grunts.' That Boyle was alright for a college boy. Your old man rigged up some bandage straps to sling that baby up on his shoulder."

That's as far as Tony gets in his story before he's got to take a piss.

He walks out to the tree line with his Zippo and Zig Zags.

Tomorrow's Good Friday. We got half a day of school, but most of us won't be there. I must've seen about half the guys in my class here—Chris, Jay, and Paul and a few more. It's so dark, who knows who else is out there. I already got one turn with the hip waders. I was out there a good hour or more. The old man and I went to the shallows, but it still was up to my thighs. After a while, you really start to feel the cold in the water, even with the waders. I got my gloves and winter coat on, but there's no way to keep your clothes dry when you're half a net deep in smelt. I can really feel the chill now, out of the water. Dipping works up a sweat, especially when they're running good. One pull, the net was so heavy, almost took me downstream. Dad was close by again, but even strong as he is, I wonder if he could've got me in time if I fell. "Keep your head up and your back straight, less you want to take a dip," he said. I filled the bucket myself a couple times, the catch shining like Coors Light cans in the headlights of the old Ford. When the five-gallon bucket filled again, it was Johnny's turn in the waders, so now I do the dumping. Three black trash bags sit almost full in the truckbed.

The music's quieter now that most of the party crowd's gone. Only the serious dippers and drunks stick around this late. The slow breeze in from the bay is just cold enough to frost my neck and give me goosebumps on my arms. The spot on the river where we're at's got a tree on the other side, growing sideways out the bank. It swings back and forth real slow over the brown water like an old man in a rocking chair. It's not so crowded on the bank now that most the traffic's gone. Uncle Tony's still smoking with Chester Wolff out by the maples on the other side of the road. The moonlight's bright enough now I can see their faces. They're both real serious—probably talking about Lacey again. She left him on Christmas Day, and he still breaks down every time he talks about her. There's nothing like a six-foot-three, two-hundred-fifty-pound Italian-Mexican with a big bushy moustache, fifth of Popov in hand, rolling around in the dirt crying like a baby in his leather Harley jacket.

When it happens, about once a week or so, Dad's quick to point out that even though Tony's like a brother, he's not blood.

Tommy and Ryan sleep in the cab of the pick-up. Their blanket is the canvas tarp strip Dad uses to cover his tools in the truck bed. Ryan's mouth is open like a smelt sucking for water. Tommy's curled up like a bear cub. Rest of the guys took a break from the river. Dad's chugging Old Milwaukee with my baseball coach, Mr. Roth. They're drunk laughing by the cooler in the back. Johnny plays catch with Roth's kid. His name's Johnny, too. They're both fifth graders but the Roth kid's a fat little fuck. My brother Johnny's skinny like me. People always say we look like twins but I'm taller, older.

Colonel Henry and Grandma Clio used to come out here every year, long as I can remember. Never showed up this year, though. They're not big into dipping smelt, but they sit around the fire, drink beer, and smoke with the best of 'em. Last year they got here around one in the morning with some hot plates of pulled pork, mashed potatoes, brown beans, and barbecue sauce. Must be five in the morning now, and I'm starving. The venison sandwiches and can of brown beans we had are long gone now. There's a part of me that keeps thinking any minute the Colonel's Lincoln's gonna turn down the path to find our spot on the river. Colonel Henry will light his cigar, take off that beaver-skin hat, and scratch his head while he tells me in Kentucky drawl to help Grandma with the food in the backseat. Their dinner leftovers will warm my hands through the foil Grandma wrapped around the plates, and I'll feel that hot air from inside the car, just before it slips out into the dark morning frost, and my face will remember what it felt like to not be outside, to not be here.

The only headlights we see for now are headed out to Mackinac Trail.

The night's catch steams in silver piles from buckets and trash bags in the bed of Dad's truck. A few smelt flop around in small empty spaces in the back. Some are just there, frozen to the wood on the bed. I love smelt dipping, but I hate that fish stink, and smelt, in these numbers, can do some real damage to your nostrils. It's that cold, muddy fish smell that grocery store fish can't match. The way they're piled up there, I'm not sure how we're gonna get back home, all six of us, without somebody sitting on a pile of fish. We really killed 'em tonight. There'll be smelt frying for weeks.

There's no good reason for me to go back down to the river, but I've got an urge to get down there one more time and feel the little scaly darts pull the net downcurrent. Dad and Tony found a campfire ring. They're smoking by the fire, roasting a couple smelt. Dad moves the stick to different spots in the pit to keep the little silver fish from burning. All three younger boys are sleeping in the cab of the truck, the windows fogged from their snoring. They all got mud on their jackets and pants. Ryan and Tommy got their sweatshirt hoods and gloves on. Johnny's wearing Dad's camouflage Budweiser cap with the brim loose over his eyes and nose. The cab smells like smelt, sweat, and wet sand when I open up the truck for another trash bag.

"You going back down?" Dad asks me.

"We got enough damn smelt already, dude." Tony puffs and chokes a little on his joint. "It's not all about the fish."

"No, but the fishing makes it better," my old man says. "Come sit down, Buck. You're old enough to hear this."

I want to go back to the river. See the smelt caught in the steel mesh and feel the cold numb of the steel net through my brown jersey gloves. The icy water of the Carp feels safer, warmer than Tony and Dad's cold faces over the fire pit. Dad points for me to stay put, so I take my seat on a half slab of birch that'll feed the fire before dawn.

"Your Grampa was a good man," says Tony. "Gave me work and a place to stay when we got back from the war. I'd do anything for him."

"Can't do anything for him now, Uncle Tony," I say, feeling my chest ice up. "He's gone. Nobody gonna bring him back."

"He ain't coming back, but we sure's hell gonna do something about it," Dad says. "That's my old man. You listen to me and listen good, boy—I don't want you telling no one about this, not your mother, nobody. You got me?" His hazel eyes burn through my frosted soul. All I can do is nod and look down at the roots that stick out through the last few patches of ice.

Last year, out here at the Carp, the Colonel got into it good with Uncle Ray about church and God. Uncle Ray was talking about how Colonel Henry and Grandma Clio should just get married already, instead of living in sin. When Ray brought it up, made me sick to my gut. I never wanted to think about Grandma and Henry rolling around wrinkled and naked. Why would old people even want sex—leave the fucking to the young. Ray must've been thinking a lot about it though. Brought it up a few times before the Colonel told him to shut his "got-damned mouth." Colonel Henry always says, "Ain't no bigger hypocrites than you'll find in church on Sunday, boy. Biggest sinners of 'em all." He gave old Ray an earful, and Ray mostly stood there shaking his head.

Everybody knows Grandma Clio is the boss, but she let Henry go on, shooting Ray bad looks. Never seen Colonel Henry get so many words out without

Grandma stopping him, but she was pissed off at Ray. Let old Henry lay into him. Seemed like every other word was a curse, but the Colonel cranks it up when he gets riled. Ray said something about blasphemy, and the Colonel told him why should he care about a god who let him sit there and watch three of his brothers die in a coal mine. "What kind of deity kills children and ruins the life of a nine-year-old boy?" he asked Ray. Henry and five of his brothers fell in the shaft but only two made it out. "What the hell kind a faith a boy have in a god that cruel?" Henry told us how he never went to church after that. All this is probably the reason Ray didn't come out this year. Don't know why the Colonel and Grandma Clio didn't come though. They patch fights over a bottle of scotch—never take anything too personal. Wherever they are, it's got to be warmer than here.

I wish I could go back and erase everything Tony and Dad told me about their revenge plan. I wish I was one of the younger boys, sleeping in the cab of the truck, even with all the stink. Lester Cronin's got it coming, but I never wanted to be drug into killing, even if it's for Grandpa. Makes sense now why Tony's keeping such a close eye on Lester. No surprise he's the one who's gonna take him down.

I'm sure it's personal, too—not just about Grandpa. Tony's still sore over the walleye contest. They say old Cronin cheated—caught fish after the deadline. Nobody could prove anything, the contest being on the honor system and all, but everybody knows Lester Cronin caught almost a pound after the deadline was over—stole second place and Tony's hundred-fifty-dollar prize. Before Lacey left, that was all Tony would talk about when he got pissed-off drunk.

Tony got real fumed last week when Mom told him what happened with Lester's mother. Rumor is Lester killed her off with D-Con. Needed the inheritance money so he could keep his hardware store open. Rat poisoned her every day till she croaked. Nobody in town can prove that either, but everybody knows the truth.

I zip down my fly and piss by Dad's front truck tire. Try to get my jeans all the way back up while I walk past the fogged windows of the old Ford, north of the fire, but the zipper jams and pinches my pointing finger. When I get the zipper up, I suck the blood from my finger and grab that smelt net one more time. Walk the path down the hill to the river. Don't even look back up the ridge when somebody tries to start the truck. Could be that Tony and Dad had enough and are packing up, but it might be they're trying to keep the boys warm in the cab or to keep the battery from draining in the cold. The radio was on all night and half the morning so it needs a good charge.

The dim sunlight fights its way up from behind the birches and maples and paints a pink-red sky. Hard sand from the bank falls in chunks when I step in the wrong places. I feel drunk, but I didn't touch any alcohol this time—not even a sniff of Dad or Tony's beer. The truck motor still won't start. It sounds like a hacksaw in rookie hands. After a few tries, somebody finally gets the engine to turn over. The eight-track is blasting up on the ridge behind me. Sounds like Styx again. About three feet down, a big chunk of hard sand crumbles off the side. I try to grab the branches of the pine that grows crooked, almost sideways over the water, but it only keeps me up for a few more seconds. The tip of the tree bounces back like a slingshot, slapping me in the face.

* * *

The current pushes me away from the hill-top campsite where Dad's truck is parked. I don't yell, not even with the shock of the cold water. It's not that deep, and I'm sure somebody heard the splash. I can't see anybody, just the cold red sunrise and the roots and trees that stick out the steep bank of the Carp. I try to pull myself out but my clothes are too heavy. The hip waders fill fast with river and it's all I can do to breathe, to keep my head above the dark water. The river thrashes me to a branch sticking out the right side bank hill. I grab the twisted cedar with frost-numb fingers. I think of Cody LeVassuer's cold, white and blue carcass. I'm stronger than him. I won't die in this river. The cold's loosening my grip, though, and the wet's prying my fingers from the branch. I hold on a good couple of minutes, then I give in and go where the river wants to take me. I fight with all the fight left in me to get back to the bank, but the water's too heavy. I paddle my arms and kick my legs, with nothing left but my adrenaline. My body gives out so I rest a few seconds and try to do it again, but all the muscle in my arms and legs is gone. I'm scared when my head goes under but it feels kind of peaceful, in a way, 'cause I'm so tired.

Last summer, a couple months after Henry and Ray's big fight, Dad and old Henry got into some deep bullshitting when we were cooking burgers and brats out at the dunes. Henry says he's mostly an atheist, but he could be wrong. There could be a God—nobody knows for sure. Guess that's the best anybody's got to go with. Doesn't calm me much, not knowing what's next, but the river's taking me down, taking me with her, and nothing I do can change that. My head gives way to the Carp's brown current.

After the other boys fell asleep, Tony finished his Army story. He said that him and Dad took turns carrying the baby girl, but Dad carried it more than Tony.

"Don't know how he did it," Tony said, "humping the sixty and all. My fat ass had a hard enough time without the baby, but I tried to pull my weight."

He said that the baby was good luck. Not a shot was fired the three days they carried that baby. They fed her water and coffee through a green nipple they rigged up out of rain gear.

"You would've thought it was a real tit the way that baby would suck on that thing," Tony said. "We left it with a little girl the first village we come across. Humped a good thirty miles that day and then the shit got real hot. Took three, no, four KIA in our platoon alone in a roadside ambush the next day. Can you believe that, Buck?" He told me. "A baby, right there, in the middle of the fucking jungle."

A single hand rips me out of the river with a pull like a steel crane. That kind of force, it's got to be Uncle Tony. All I feel is the hand and the suction of the river, until the iced air stings through my soaked clothes and works its way to my head. I feel punching on my chest, steady and strong till I chunk out water. Everything feels hard and real again. Then I see the face with the hands. It's Dad, not Tony. "Gonna be a cold ride home," he says. "Told you keep your head up. Got to keep your goddamn head up, boy."

Winner of the 2012 Boulevard Short Fiction Contest for Emerging Writers.

Demolition
Steven Huff

That summer we tore out the whole bridge deck.
It was supposed to be work,
but we laughed like horses, jitterbugged
with the jackhammers. We chiseled out
the rotted concrete chunks under our shoes,
calling them by the various names
of cheaters we knew: Those home-busting
cowbirds who now kept their beer
in our old fridges, slept with our women, splashed
our cologne on their sticky faces in the morning.
This was some years before a doctor taught me
to manage my fury like a checking account, spend
some in one direction, more in another; long before
those arts-and-crafts lessons in the nuthouse
where I built a wooden hat rack for my wife.
But Jesus, how we pound-pounded that bridge,
watched the concrete chunk-a-chunks
tumble through corroded rebar rods,
dropping thunk-a-*boom* to the gully below.

An American Uncle
Steven Huff

Most Americans I know had an uncle like yours who
drove a red car with a leaky gas tank that burned up
one afternoon when some woman leaned on it and lit her
cigarette. He played poker and screwed, this uncle.
You had other uncles who screwed and nothing much
happened, but locusts rose from the abyss when this uncle
screwed and the bells in town went clunk. You found him
lying on the couch one morning, his face a raincloud-blue,
and you asked your mom as you dressed for school,
Is he dead? And she said, Why, no, *no*, though you could tell
she wasn't too sure. This uncle wrestled the devil away
from the door of your house—he was the only one around
who could do such a thing, and when they tumbled over
the grass they threw off jagged splinters of light. He was
named for a Civil War general, but he didn't care. When he
wasn't lying deathly on the couch he was pouring cement
for a dam in Ecuador or Idaho. He coaxed you into
reading *Ulysses* and he called you up from Bora-Bora to ask
if you'd finished it yet, and he knew you were lying. In the war
he was shot down over France, and he parachuted into
a whorehouse. He taught you to love Billy Holliday
and Roosevelt. Unhappy women took turns marrying him
and each of them knew all the others. Your uncle who
never lived anywhere in particular as far as you knew,
he never loved anyone but your mother and you
and somebody else who probably never was born.
Which is what made him an American uncle, I suppose.

Some Get-Back
Eric Miles Williamson

I'd been restricted to the trailer for hitting my
brother. The entire summer holed-up in a rusty,
nineteen-foot Airstream trailer next to the Mohawk
station where Pop worked. There was no escape,
because he was sure to catch me if I tried to leave. No
privileges: I could only go outside to empty the toilet's
holding tank.

I discovered a lot that summer.

I discovered pot, thanks to my friend, Hiro, who'd
sneak me joints through the plastic porthole near the
rear of the trailer. I discovered acid. I discovered, in
Pop's decanters, Scotch. I discovered mushrooms. I
discovered a jazz radio station. I discovered, while
reading the letter my mother sent me, that she had
been saved by Jesus. I discovered, in the same letter,
that my mother had played second clarinet in
elementary school, and that's why I was a good
trumpet player. I discovered, from that letter, that
everything I'd ever done good in my life was because
of her, and everything I'd done lame was the fault of
Pop.

From the Funk & Wagnall's encyclopedia set I kept
stashed in the drawers beneath and above my bed, I
learned that every scientific theory except the ones we
believe in now has been proven false. I learned that if
you divide a second in half, and then in half again,
and again and again, you can divide it forever, and
therefore there's an infinity between every tick on a

watch. I learned that you can know where you are, or how fast you are going, but not both. I learned that you can't predict the path of a quark, and therefore everything in the cosmos is unpredictable.

I decided I didn't care about not getting any nookie. I decided I was going to live in the woods in Oregon when I left Oakland and shoot animals and build a log cabin and kill anyone who came near me. I decided my mother must have mated with an intelligent milkman when Pop was at work and produced the zygote that became me, because there was not a chance in hell I was borne of the ape who was allegedly my progenitor. I decided, after reading about Marx, that I was a communist.

I grew ten inches and twenty pounds, and went from being fat-boy to being a monster. Every day of the summer I did pushups for an hour in the morning and an hour at night. I did hundreds of sit-ups each day before noon. I put my hands on the counters and did dips as if the counters were parallel bars. Veins popped out of my arms and neck. I clipped my hippie hair off with a pair of tin-snips. I did a bad job on purpose. I could throw truck tires around like they were Styrofoam life preservers. I could swing the sledge against split-rims like John Henry. I had to start shaving. When I'd cut myself I'd just let the blood run down my neck.

I could hardly wait for school to start.

There were some people I wanted to talk to.

It was the end of summer, it was hot, and the shit stank fierce. I was emptying the holding tank one bucket of chemical-green shit at a time, I was carrying the buckets around the back of the Mohawk station and dumping them in the Ladies Room toilet, I was paying my friend Hiro half of my allowance to help, when the idea came to me.

Even though I was a fat-boy, I was one of the best athletes at Jack London Junior High, because every day for many years I'd been running home from school being chased by herds of cawing Mexicans and blacks. I was no sprinter, fat-boy me, but I could run my fastest without ever slowing down. I could run for hours at full-tilt. If I got a couple minutes' head start, I could get home to the Mohawk station without being touched. When they caught me, though, they beat me bloody. All of my fingers have been broken from being stomped on. I have an ugly nose. One kid sliced me up so bad I got sixty-eight stitches. I limped for six months when I was in sixth grade. My head's been knocked so many times, I wouldn't be surprised if I was permanently stupid.

And if I showed up at the Mohawk with tears in my eyes or limping, Pop would smack me around, too, for being a coward. Unless I could prove I'd taken one out. Proof: my own bloody knuckles.

Being a whitey isn't as easy as it seems.

When I got home, I worked out. I slung around truck tires at the Mohawk station, stacked them and restacked them. Instead of using the air gun on the lug nuts of the trucks I used a T-bar. I could lay beneath a car and hold up the tranny while someone bolted it on. I could climb the tire racks without using my feet.

But I wanted to make sure not to get the shit kicked out of me by Pop for being a coward. So sometimes—hell, lots of times—I ripped up my knuckles on the sidewalk, scraped my knuckles raw to bone so Pop would think I kicked some ass. I'd have dangling chunks of skin I could flap back over the meat. I'd grind them up good.

I was too chicken to ever hit the Mexicans and the

blacks back. I was too chicken because every time I'd hit one of my own brothers, Pop had beaten the shit out of me. "You're bigger than they are," he said. And then he popped me. "That's what it feels like when someone bigger hits you." The thought of hitting someone had always terrified me. My brothers, Clyde and Kent, could cry at will. They could just be standing there pumping gas or scooping dogshit with the shovel and if they felt like it they could just break out in sobs and tears. "T-Bird hit me," they'd say. I'd deny the charge, and get popped double for lying as well as for beating up my brothers.

Pop had two rules.
    1. Take one out with you.
    2. *Remember.*
"Never, never forget," he said. "You keep a list. Your 'Get-Back' list."

He reached behind the marble-topped counter in the shop and pulled out an old pad of paper. He showed it to me. The words were written in pencil, faded and smeared and smudged with grease and oil, and on the pad was a list of names, with columns, and the columns were "Date" and "Offense."

"A list," he said.

I noticed my mother's name was on the list. In capital letters. Big.

His father's name was on the list.

His boss' name.

Nixon and Agnew.

The offenses were vague: Shame. Too many. The Night. Cops. A woman's name.

The dates went back to before I was born.

"Never, *never* forget. Never. You keep a list, so you can be sure. And before you get even, you wait until *they* have forgotten what they did to *you*. Then there's two ways to proceed," he said. "One: remind them of what they did to you when you're nailing them."

And then Pop looked up from beneath the hood of the car he'd been working on, and he smiled big and his eyes shimmered with joy, "And Two: make them *think* you're doing them a favor while you're destroying them. Someday, when they're groveling, when they're drooling on themselves and vomiting in the gutter, when they have the gun to their heads and they're ready to check out, they'll look back and know it was *you* who orchestrated everything, you who were the puppeteer, you who were pulling their strings. And when they pull the trigger anyway, and they know it was you that brought them to this, then, *THEN* you have proper get-back. It might take you ten, maybe twenty years to get the right and perfect chance to shell out some get-back. But remember, get-back isn't worth the while unless it's forever, unless it's the *final payment*."

Pop put his list back under the counter, and he stood there for a second with a blank face, stood there as if time had stopped and he were somewhere else, as if he had vanished. And then his lips began slowly to curl and twist, to slide upwards on his face and into a smile and he said, slowly and with a voice that sounded like the first time he'd used his true voice instead of making sounds he'd thought he wanted people to hear, "Payment," he said. "*Payment in full.*"

I kept a list. It was a long list. It could take me the rest of my life if I waited for the right moments. I would never be bored.

Pop was on my list.

***

Things weren't much better for Hiro, since he was Japanese, and a shrimp. When we were running home, we'd split up, we'd use specially designed escape routes, we'd hide in warehouses and in tunnels beneath the railroad tracks and we'd duck into corner markets and try to wait the Mexicans and blacks out. But it didn't matter to them how late they got home from school. No one was waiting for them anyway. They didn't even know who their parents were.

So Hiro was a Japanese shrimp, I was a fat-boy whitey, we both wore black-rimmed glasses, and there was no way either of us was ever going to get any nookie. Nookie was almost something mythological. It was something I'd never get. The school's fat-boy four-eyed punching bag is not the likeliest candidate for nookie. I asked six different girls, four Marias and two Lucys to the seventh grade dance. Five of them said no, and Maria Luna thought it was so hilarious and ridiculous that *I'd* asked *her*, that she went into the cafeteria ahead of me and told everyone. When I walked through the doors, everyone was laughing. I mean they were really laughing. They were choking on their food laughing. They were having a good old time.

Maria Luna went on my list.

Kids coming home from school had seen me going in and out of the trailer next to the Mohawk station. They were on welfare, but at least they had apartments. I was trailer-trash that didn't even live in a trailer park. And they'd seen me emptying the buckets of slimy green, chemically-treated turds. Someone would spot me, and then they'd round up all the kids they knew, and soon I'd have an audience, all of them laughing and holding their noses and squatting along the sidewalk as if they were dropping loads for me to haul away to the Ladies Room toilet.

The ass-kickings were the worst when report cards came out. At Jack London Junior High, if you got caught with A's on your report card, the beating was especially bad, and then the ridicule that followed was even worse. The girls? They didn't want nerds: they wanted real men, men who could protect them at the laundromat when they were washing the family clothes, men who were already sixteen and had Camaros and Firebirds and Monte Carlos. And we had plenty of sixteen year olds in the eighth grade, kids who couldn't speak much English, kids who'd flunked plenty of grades. Our basketball team was ten kids, six-foot mutants—virtual retards—with drivers licenses and stringy goatees. Our team would scare the shit out of the other teams, showing up for games in their Bondo-mobiles, all of them drunk, making sure that at least five of them fouled-out each game, and fouled-out in style. They used to send the opposing teams home bloody. One of the local schools—from the fancy side of town—wouldn't even come to play our team. They'd forfeit every time we came up on the schedule. The more our school's goons flunked out, the better they were in sports, since each year they stayed behind, they got another year older than the other kids. Hiro and me got younger every year, and the odds of us getting any nookie when everyone else was six feet tall and drove cars and smoked pot and snorted coke and had good part-time jobs at the canneries and UPS and the loading docks surrounding the rim of the bay—the odds of getting laid if you were a little whitey fat-boy who got A's in school were nil. Zip. How can you compete with those kinds of guys? At my school, flunking was the epitome of cool. So when report cards came out, Hiro and I would be absent.

I'd grown, though. I had grown, and I had a list.

Emptying those buckets of shit, the kids from my class watching as the green slop lapped onto my blue jeans, the sky Oakland gray and the breeze curling and twisting and eddying around the courtyard of the Mohawk station's brick-surrounded lot—cigarette wrappers swirling and me and Hiro dodging dog turds as we walked through the alley behind the station with the plastic buckets so heavy our shoulders drooped— emptying those buckets and watching the faces of the kids, the girls, two of whom I'd asked to the seventh grade dance and who'd rejected me, I decided what must be done, and to whom, and just how—and how splendidly—it would be done.

I was a kid with a plan.

I was glad when school started. The only kids who recognized me were the ones who came every Saturday to the shop to watch me empty the buckets of turds. I had cuts on my face and my hair was so short I didn't need to comb it and I was bigger than everyone by twenty or thirty pounds. Some of the flunkees were taller than me—Joe Gonzalez, Joe Borges, Joseph Alvarez—but they were skinny dudes with sunken chests and pointy heads. I could take them out in a flat second.

And they knew it. When I walked down the hall, my hair shorn ragged like Cro-Magnon Man, and my arms pumped up like hamhocks, people kept out of my way. And I liked it that way, and I encouraged it— I made my eyes look crazy. My eyes are gray like old plaster. I made them look creepier, though. I kept my eyes wide open and bulging like I was insane, like I'd never before blinked them and never would again. I had dry eyes that looked like they saw something beyond the world out there, something that would spook normal people but that I was in cahoots with.

Number one on my list was Alphonso. Alphonso Joseph San Miguel.

So I made it my personal mission to make friends with him.

I'd read this book by a Chinese writer named Sun-Tzu that Hiro had loaned me. It was his father's book. His father had been in the relocation camps in World War II, and he was six-foot five and over two hundred pounds and there wasn't a person on the planet that could look at him without knowing that if they crossed him they'd pay *the final payment.* Even his name, Shig, sounded like an ancient Japanese weapon, like a sickle or a sacred spear used to ram enemies. You could tell that he'd dice you up clean and nifty, and he wouldn't do a victory dance afterwards, no—he'd stand up straight and he'd pull out a handkerchief and he'd wipe the blade clean and walk slowly away, as if he'd just found a good parking place downtown and paralleled without nudging a bumper.

When Hiro handed me Sun-Tzu, he said, "Read this."

"Books are for queers," I said.

"Not this one," Hiro said. "Look," and he turned to an dog-eared page.

Make the enemy's road long and torturous, the underlined paragraph read. *Lure him along it by baiting him with easy gains.*

"And this," Hiro said, and he showed me another passage.

Know the other, know yourself, and the victory will not be at risk. Know the ground, know the natural conditions, and the victory will be utter.

I nodded. "Sounds good to me."

"It's my father's favorite book," Hiro said. "He

keeps it on the nightstand in his bedroom. He gave me a copy after the Chavez brothers pounded us last year. He gave me a copy of the book and a new chess set."

So I swiped a copy of my own from the Oakland Public Library downtown, and during my summer on restriction, when I wasn't working out, and I read the book over and over. *The Art of War. The Art of War. The Art of War. The Art of War.* I nearly memorized the sucker.

The first item of business when school started was to lull my enemies, to infiltrate their camp, to make them believe I was *one of them.*

I set out to make friends with Alphonso.

Lunchtime the first day of school, I walked up to his table in the cafeteria and sat down.

"This table isn't for faggot *culeros,*" he said. "*Puta madre mojón gringo maricón.*"

He looked at me. The other Mexicans looked down at their sloppy joes and coleslaw.

"Maybe *you,*" I said, "should leave. You know, I saw your mother on San Pablo Boulevard," I said, "with the other whores," and before I knew it he was across the table with his hands around my neck.

But I was ready for him. I'd rolled pennies from Pop's change bucket and my fists banging on his head were like hammers. It only took two punches to knock him dizzy and sprawling across the slop on the table. He looked up at me, and his eyes were twitching. He was breathing funny.

I took the rolls of pennies from my fists and peeled the paper and sprinkled the pennies over his face.

The cafeteria was silent.

I leaned close to his ear.

"Together," I said, "we can kick some holy ass."

* * *

After school, when I was walking through the parking lot toward home, I saw Alphonso. He was standing next to his '68 GTO. He was only in seventh grade, and I was in eighth, but he was three years older, and had his driver's license.

"T-Bird," he said. "Come over here. I'm needing to talk some words with you."

I walked over to his GTO. It was bondo-gray and had a set of Krager mags and 50-series monster BF Goodrich tires on the back, 60's in the front, raised whites.

He opened the passenger door. I got in.

"I could cut you up like a pig," he said. "Like a gringo pig."

We drove.

"My little goat the *cabron* has a four-barrel Holley double-pumper, traction bars, and glass-packs," he said. "I got the upholstery done in TJ."

The diamond-tuck job was crushed-red velvet. *Everything* was diamond-tucked. The door panels, the glove compartment, the dashboard, even the floorboards. The inside of the trunk was diamond-tucked. It was a serious car.

"I builded the fucker my own self, the fucker," Alphonso said. "My little Goat, my *cabron*."

"It's boss," I said. I pulled a joint from my wallet. "Thai stick," I said.

"Panama Red," he said, and he took a joint from his shirt pocket and he lit it and smoked, then passed the joint to me. He smiled, and smoke leaked out from where one of his teeth was missing.

"How do you know so much about cars?" I said. "My pop works in a gas station and I live next door to it, and I don't know half as much as you."

I passed the joint back. I was getting stoned, and I felt good. I almost forgot I was sitting in a car with

Alphonso Joseph San Miguel.

Rumor had it he'd killed someone.

He leaned his head back and exhaled. We smoked with the windows rolled up so we could inhale the clouds over and over. The windows were crusted yellow with pot tar. I scraped my fingernail against the windshield, and rolled a brown ball of resin between my fingers.

"I work at Santos Rentals," Alphonso said. "Seven dollars a hour. I can fix anything made of metal."

And that's the way it went for a month. Every day after school we'd smoke a joint in Alphonso's Goat, and we'd tell stories about our families. I told Alphonso how my mother used to ride with the Hell's Angels, and *he* thought that was *really* cool. I told him how my father used to play trumpet in the Oakland symphony, and he told me how his grandfather used to play violin in a mariachi band in Mexico. He told me how his father was illegal, and how his father and his uncle shared a green card between them, how sometimes he'd have to stay at his uncle's apartment for a month at a time when the federales were getting feisty, and he'd have to pretend that his uncle was his father and his aunt was his mother. He told me how some day he wanted to build dragsters himself, how he wanted to make the world's lightest rail so the horsepower/weight ratio alone would compensate for any problems he might encounter with aerodynamics.

One weekend, when he didn't have to go to work, we drove out to Berkeley and walked out to the end of the Berkeley Pier to smoke a joint. We stayed there until sunset, the bay shimmering orange and purple, the fog in the distance matted atop the Golden Gate and San Francisco. You could hear the seagulls crying happy over the garbage dumps, and you could hear the tugboats hooting their foghorns. A pelican dove into the water and came up with a fish and slowly lifted itself into the air, flapping hard and heavy. A yacht slowly slipped past, and the people on it were having a party, dancing on the deck and throwing their empty champagne glasses into the water. They looked really happy.

"My papa's a wetback," he said. "In Mexico, he was an engineer. He went to the college in Mexico City and he designed bridges gringo tanks rolls across when the Mexicans buy them and bring them home. But when he gets to America and tries to become the engineer, they make him go to junior college to get the American credentials, the gringo papers. He failed that fucking freshman English every time he taked it, every motherfucking time, every semester for ten years, twenty times he took freshman fucking English, twenty times he fucking flunked. His *English* not good enough to build *bridges*? His *English* not good enough to draw *blueprints*? His fucking *Ingles?* Fuck college. Fuck the fucking college and the fucking school. So he's just a wetback. But I'm not. I'm not a wetback because my papa worked hard all his life to hide from the *federales*. In Mexico he was a government inspector, he was a boss, he told people what was right and what was wrong. Here, in the fucking America, he's a garbage fucking man."

Alphonso looked out at the yacht and shook his head.

"When you throw something away, my father is the *pinche mierda* that picks it fucking up," he said.

"I'm sorry," I said.

"Don't be sorry for me. I'm no fucking wetback, and I can fix anything made of metal. And I'm going to make the fastest dragster ever *did* the quarter mile.

My childrens will be motherfucking proud of their papa *reata*."

The fog was sweeping toward us. The sun behind had set. The bay clicked from orange and purple and red to battleship gray. We stood silent a long time.

"You know," he said. "Even though you a fucking gringo and you get A's and shit in school, you okay, man. In my book, you okay."

I shouldn't have felt flattered, but I did.

I still had plans. In P.E. the first fall sport was wrestling. Wrestling was especially suited to my needs.

For wrestling, Coach Butler made us weigh-in on the scales while he noted down the numbers on a pad. There were only three guys heavier than me, all of them fat-boys, geeky nerd friends of mine—Nelson Van Sickle, my science partner; Chaim Goldstein, the school whiz at anything that had to do with math; and Load Hansen, who played tuba in band. All two hundred pounders. Coach Butler grouped the four of us together, and we were *#1 Mat*. As your weight got lighter, you moved down mats, all the way down to *#15 Mat*. The goal was to move up mats by beating the people at your starting mat. If you were a loser, you moved down mats and wrestled lighter and lighter kids, until you got to *#15*, where the runts were, Tito Campos, Joe Garcia, Joseph Guiterrez, and my friend Hiro. Since I was on *#1 Mat*, my job was to fend off challengers.

That's not what I had in mind, though.

Master Sun said, *Better to seem to lose the battle and actually win, than to seem to win the battle and actually lose. Sometimes the seeming loser is in truth the victor. One must know the definition of victory before one engages the enemy.*

I won by losing.

Everyone on my list was on a mat beneath mine, and so, to get to them, I had to lose.

During wrestling month, I'd pretend to wrestle, and then let myself get pinned, and down a mat I'd go. Until I met with someone on my list, someone who'd pummeled me years before, sometimes someone who'd knifed me or stuck my head in a toilet four or five years before, and when I got to them on the mat, I'd crush them. I'd smash their face into the mat with my forearm against the back of their neck, I'd twist their arms behind their backs until they screamed so loud that everyone else stopped wrestling and Coach Butler had to pull me off.

I got sent to Mr. Hanover, the Vice Principal, who told me that I was a rough ball of clay, and it was education's job to shave off the rough edges.

When I got all the way down to *#12 Mat*, I met up with Francisco Alvarez, who only weighed ninety pounds. We were in "referee position," Francisco on his knees and me behind him, and I whispered into his ear, "You remember in fourth grade when you punched me in the mouth in basketball practice?"

"No," he said.

"You chipped one of my front teeth," I said. "You don't remember? I had to go to the doctor?"

"I don't remember," he said.

"I do."

When Coach Butler blew the start whistle, I picked Francisco up into the air over my head and slammed him down so hard I knocked him unconscious. Coach Butler had to slap him around to get him to come to.

And when he came to, I was standing over him, smiling.

I started a trend. Everyone started losing. No one cared about winning anymore. All the fat-boys, all the big nerds and geeks, started losing and moving down the mats to the lower mats and pounding the runts when they got there, following their enemies from mat to mat by losing and winning as necessary. It got so bad, with no one really caring about winning or losing, that Coach Butler had to cancel wrestling and move us to weight lifting, where we wouldn't have to touch each other.

We didn't get to play football that season.

But I got to cross six names off my list.

Alphonso helped out a lot, too. It was like having my own private hit man.

"Anyone fucking with T-Bird Murphy," he said, "fucking with Alphonso. I don't care how old we are, and where we living, if the motherfucker fucks with you, he fucks with Alphonso. And if you don't tell me, you, too, fucking with Alphonso."

All I had to do was say that someone had looked at me cross-eyed, and it didn't matter if it was one of his other friends or not, he'd shred them. I was helping Alphonso with his homework, and he was teaching me about cars and engines and electrical systems and fuel combustion, and if anyone fucked with either of us, they were meat. So I'd put the finger on a kid who'd thrown a football at the back of my head in sixth grade, and Alphonso would break his finger or slap him rummy in front of his friends. I could have asked Alphonso to assassinate someone, and he would have done it for me, his *amigo gringo*.

On my way to school one morning, as I was walking through the shop to put back the dogshit shovel, Pop pulled me aside. He was working under the hood of an old Chrysler Newport.

"The toilet in the trailer stinks like shit," Pop said.

"Sorry," I said. "I forgot the chemicals this week."

"Sorry," Pop said. "Empty the fucker."

"After school," I said.

"Notice you have a new friend," Pop said. He slipped the wrench and banged his knuckles against the manifold. "Son of a bitch," he said. Blood seeped through the grease on Pop's knuckles. "Son of a bitch."

"He's not really a friend," I said. I rolled up my sleeve and showed Pop my scar. "You remember when I got this?"

"Sixty-eight stitches," Pop said.

"Alphonso," I said. "My new friend."

Pop smirked. He smirked and looked at me over his glasses and he just stared at me, smirking. And then his smirk widened into a grin, a full smile, both rows of teeth showing. "Get out of here," he said, and I looked back before I turned the corner and saw Pop, and he was standing in the middle of the lube bay, wiping down his hands with a red rag, and he was watching me, and he was still smiling.

Things around Jack London Junior High had changed for me lately. I still had my geeky friends, and we still did all the geek things together—chess club, band, California Junior Scholarship Federation meetings, study-group at lunchtime, drama club. But now no one else would talk to me. They wouldn't even *look* at me. When they'd see me coming down the hall, they'd look down at the floor and they'd back off, scattering. The school seemed much more spacious.

In P.E., I could do just about anything I wanted.

During basketball, I didn't mind fouling out, and so when I had the ball, I'd just run over anyone in my way and do a lay-up. Rebounding, I'd swing my arms and elbows, and one time I smacked a Jarimallo so hard in the mouth that he bit off the inside of his cheek. There was blood everywhere, and I got sent to the Vice Principal's office again.

"You're a straight-A student," he said. "Why are you doing this?"

"Doing what?"

"Fighting all the time, doing what," he said.

"They're the thugs," I said. "They've been beating the hell out of all of us for years now. You know that."

Mr. Hanover shook his head.

"You can't just run around taking justice into your own hands," he said.

"Where's the justice supposed to come from, then?"

"Justice?" he said. "*Justice?* How long have you lived in this country, justice."

He stood up. He walked over to my chair and put his hand on my shoulder. He lowered his voice. "Look," he said. "I don't give a damn what you do to the little shits."

I looked up at him.

"Just don't do it on school property."

He sent me home for the day. When I walked past the idiot math class, I peeked in and caught Alphonso's eye. He asked for a hall-pass and came out to meet me.

"Suspended," I said.

"No big," he said. "Why?"

"Nailed a Jarimallo."

Alphonso nodded in approval. "Fucking bueno."

"I have to do some work on the trailer," I said.

"Pop wants me to fix the shower pump, and I don't know what the hell to do."

"Let's go," Alphonso said. "I will help you."

Alphonso parked his Goat next to the trailer.

"You *live* here?"

"And my father and my two brothers."

"Fuck," Alphonso said. "I didn't know."

"Didn't know what?"

"I didn't know gringos," he said, and he fished for a word or two, "I didn't know gringos were poor, too."

"Let's fix that pump," I said. "I'll go get the toolbox."

Pop stopped me. "What are you doing home from school?"

"Alphonso's going to help me empty the holding tank, and in return I told him he could use your tools to work on his car for a while. Please?"

"If I need them, that's the end of playtime with the tools."

I wheeled Pop's huge red Snap-On toolboxes through the lube bay and around the side of the station to the trailer. Alphonso was smoking a cigarette.

"You know," Alphonso said, "I gave you your first real battle wound, didn't I?"

I rolled up my sleeve and showed him my scar.

"That's a good scar," he said. He nodded proudly. "A good fucker, that scar. I'll show you *my* first *cabroncito.*"

He lifted his T-shirt and showed me his chest. It was mapped with scars, red ones, white ones, black ones. It looked like he'd been whipped, too.

"You see this one?" he said. He drew his finger

along a small white scar the length of a tire valve. "This little fucker was my first one, and just look at the fuck. It's nothing. If I show people this scar, they think nothing. It's a pussy scar, and I got it making play-fight with my brother. No nothing in this scar. But yours," he said, and he walked over to me and lifted my shirt sleeve and ran his finger along mine— and the way he did it, the way he touched my scar, was as if he *loved* that scar, as if the scar were not a part of me but a creature living on its own in the world, a splendid and beautiful creature that Alphonso was petting, that Alphonso was in awe of— "yours is a *scar*, a scar earned in battle. Some day you will tell your childrens and your grandchildrens that you were scarred by Alphonso."

"Let's get to that pump," I said.

I showed Alphonso the part of the trailer where the problem was, underneath, and he lay on his back on the asphalt and shimmied himself between the truck tires I'd arranged that morning.

"Tight fucking fit under here," he said.

"Get your head all the way up against the tire," I said.

"Got it," he said. "It's dark, though. I can't see a fucking thing."

"I'll get you a flashlight," I said.

I wheeled the toolboxes over his legs, and I put a flashlight in his hand.

"See anything?" I said.

"It doesn't look like there's anything under here that has to do with a pump," he said.

"There's not," I said.

"What?"

"There's not," I said. "I just wanted you under the trailer, pinned."

"I don't understand."

126

"Do you understand what the word 'shit' means?"

"What the fuck you talking about?"

"When you knife little fat-boys, they don't forget," I said. "They feel like shit," I said. "They feel like this," I said, and I reached under the trailer and I pulled the handle and the shit flowed. Every shit I'd taken that week, every shit of my brothers and Pop, every turd of their girlfriends and even the turds of some of the preferred customers—slipping and sliding onto Alphonso's face.

I stood back and listened to Alphonso curse, and man did he curse. He cursed my father, my mother, my cousins, my aunts and uncles. He cursed every member of a hundred generations of Murphys. He cursed us back to Adam and his whore wife Eve.

The shit and piss and puke and spit spread out on the asphalt beneath the trailer like gurgling tar, and Alphonso kicked his legs and punched at the undercarriage of the trailer but he couldn't get loose.

Then, suddenly, his noise stopped. His legs went limp and I couldn't hear anything.

"Alphonso?" I said. "Alphonso? *Alphonso?*" But no response. "Alphonso!"

I ran to the lube bays. Pop was there, and Pete Arvey was pumping gas on the island. "There's been an accident," I said.

"What," Pop said.

"Alphonso's choking."

Pop looked at me. He winked. "Got him good?"

"Pop," I said, "he might be dead."

"Son of a bitch," Pop said. "*Son* of a *bitch*." And he called Arvey and he went to the trailer and Arvey and me followed. Pop pulled the toolboxes away, and he grabbed Alphonso's ankles and he pulled. Alphonso was limp.

"It was an accident," Pop rehearsed. "You were

emptying the tank and he got caught and he drowned. By the time you figured out what was happening, he was gone. You didn't know. It was an accident."

"It wasn't an accident," I said. "It wasn't an accident," and I slammed Alphonso's chest with my fists knotted together. He lay there corpsed. I slammed him again, and I slammed him a third time, and he coughed, and runny browned shit bubbled from his mouth and trickled down his cheeks. I sat him up and slapped his back, again, again, again, and I slapped his back again. His eyes, when they opened, couldn't see a thing.

"Alphonso," I said.

His head hung like a drunk's.

"Alphonso," I said. I slapped him. "Alphonso!"

Arvey heard the station bells ring, and went to take care of a gas customer. When he came back, he had a ten-pound sledge hoisted over his shoulder. We stood around Alphonso, Pop, Pete Arvey and me, and Alphonso stood slowly up, and he began taking off his clothes, his shirt, shoes and socks, his pants, his shorts. He stood there naked, dripping. You could see the scars on his chest through the slime. It looked like they were bubbling, like they were heated up and boiling through the shit and piss and vomit.

He walked toward us and we moved away and let him through, and he walked through the alley behind the station and cut right. A few minutes later he was back, and he'd wrapped himself in the rolling-towel from the restroom. He looked like an Incan warrior, his hair wet and slick and black, his brown skin glistening with water.

"You don't know a fucking thing about fighting, little gringo," he said. He looked each of us in the eye.

Then he stared at me. "You might be big, but you will always be a little gringo."

Pete Arvey switched his sledge hammer from one shoulder to the other.

"Tomorrow," Alphonso said, "tomorrow, my gringo fucking amigo, *I* will be clean."

And he walked off, left his Goat there next to the trailer and just walked off, buck naked under the washroom towel, walked down the street and into Oakland.

In the middle of the night I heard Alphonso's car start and drive off.

I didn't tell Hiro about what I'd done. I didn't tell anyone. Pop, though, would tell everyone who came into the station. He kept changing the story around to make it funnier—and he left out the part about nearly killing Alphonso. Once he got the story completely fixed up, he thought the Alphonso event was just about the funniest damn thing that ever happened.

For the customers, he'd put on a Mexican accent and he'd tell the story, and when he got to the end, he'd say, "Tomorrow, my gringo fucking amigo, I will be clean," over and over again, and everyone would laugh so hard their stomachs would hurt. "Tomorrow, my gringo fucking amigo, I will be clean," he said, and an old dude laughed so hard his choppers shot right out of his mouth and onto the ground. "Tomorrow, my gringo fucking amigo, my *teeth* will be clean," Pop said, and everyone laughed some more.

Alphonso never did come back to school. During Christmas break, I went by Santos Rentals, and they told me he'd quit. I didn't know where he lived, or where his uncle lived.

Eventually I started telling my own version of the

Alphonso story.

In my version, I made Alphonso beg like a coward.

In my version, I left out the part where we'd become friends.

"Some Get Back" first appeared as a chapter in *East Bay Grease*. Picador USA. 1999.

The Art of Carving
Ron Cooper

Everyone in town had at least one snapshot of the Dead End sign on the corner in front of Rondeau's Funeral Home. They kept it in a wallet or purse to flash on the road when an unsuspecting waitress asked, "Y'all on vacation?" A picture of a grinning Tag Rondeau standing under the sign graced a page in the Chamber of Commerce's brochure with the caption, "Tagmill Rondeau, Respected Businessman and Coroner." The dead-end street was hardly more than a driveway, running past the funeral home for fifty yards and stopping at the old tobacco warehouse that had been converted into the First Holiness Youth Athletic Center. Inside were a half basketball court and a weight-training area with a Nautilus machine and workout benches, which the Holiness youths would sneak to at night to do what they called premarital sets.

Some of those youths had earlier been at the purple jesus party by the river where they imbibed many, probably too many, plastic cups of that savior-named grape juice-sugar-grain alcohol concoction. They would soon weave their way to the Center, but at midnight, Purvis and Martha found no cars parked along the road, except for Rondeau's tow truck and two hearses in the garage. Purvis backed around to a set of double doors, taking care not to hit the dips in the road that might wake Martha's cousin Larson in the truck bed. The last thing Purvis needed was a retard getting in the way.

"How's our boy doing back there?" Purvis asked.

"Still out cold rolled up in that tarp. I reckon he's cozy in it. I ought to fill him up with liquor more often. You think there might be an alarm system here?"

"Alarm? Whoever breaks into a funeral parlor? We're making history."

Setting the toolbox before the double doors, Purvis shined a flashlight onto the knobs. "I ain't believing this," he said. He took a coping saw from the toolbox and removed the thin blade. "It's like they didn't want anybody breaking the lock, so they made it easy." He slid the blade between the doors, jiggled for several seconds, clamped his knuckles—not his fingertips—to a knob, and turned. "We're in."

Inside, Purvis searched the walls with the flashlight. "This is our night. Not a window in the room. We can turn on the lights and nobody'll ever know we're here."

"Let's be safe and just turn on one, just enough to find the old bastard," said Martha. She found a switch and turned on a lamp hanging directly over a stainless steel table.

"Damn! Lucky again," said Purvis. "You got the one right over the old man. That is him, ain't it?"

"I think there're only two in here. Let's just get to it."

Armey lay naked on the table. His glasses and clothes, green coveralls and everything, were wadded on the shelf below him. Purvis put a finger to Armey's bad eye. "Looks like a marble, don't it?" As Purvis looped the apron over his neck and tied it around his back, he scanned the rest of the old man's body. "Now, that's something I didn't know, that your hair, down, you know, there, gets gray. That's just pukeable ugly, especially it not circlecized. Want me to cover it up? You probably don't want to see your uncle's, you know, ding dong."

"I've seen it before," said Martha.

"I know that. You were married and all, so I know you've seen... wait, you don't mean *his*, do you?"

"We're wasting time, Purvis. You sure you know how to do this?"

Purvis searched the items on the shelf below Armey. "This'll do." He found a sock and laid it over Armey's bluish penis. "I believe in respecting the dead," said Purvis. He opened the tool box. "My old man's got chisels and saws and every damn thing in here. He's carved a whole lot of people. I mean wood people out of cypress knees, not carved up real people. He's says carving is an art. He'd have me watch him cut at the cypress knees, said carving is a good activity for bringing people together." He lifted Armey's shoulder from the table and peeked at the bullet hole in the back of the neck. "These tools ought to be able to undo a thing as well as make one. Besides, I've helped clean and butcher many a deer. You pretty much cut around the joints, give them a snap, then slice through the leaders. Might need to saw through a bone or two. Good thing is we won't need to clean and dress him. That means gut him, at least one of them does. Might be cleaning is gutting and dressing is skinning, or the other ways around, but we won't need to skin him neither. I bet that'd be hard, what with a human not having a hide like deer do."

"Just get to it." Martha felt her stomach churn. Just nerves. She could get through this. This was no worse than putting a bullet into him.

"I figure we can put the legs in one garbage bag," Purvis said, "and the arms in another, or a leg and an

133

arm together. The head and body might can go in the same one together, but I got plenty bags either way. That white eye of his, the blind one, is something, ain't it? Hell, now they're both blind." Purvis considered the woodworking tools in the bag, then turned to Martha. "Can I have my knife back now?"

Martha pulled the hawkbill from her pocket, thumbed it open, and handed it to Purvis. Without hesitation Purvis spread Armey's legs and sliced into the groin. The knife drew along so smoothly that Martha nearly thought Purvis was tracing a line with a pen, as she imagined slaughterhouse workers might do on a hanging side of beef. Purvis rolled the body to its side and drew the knife along the edge of the buttock. "Get me a bag," he said.

Shaking open a bag, Martha heard a pop. She turned back to see Purvis holding up Armey's leg like a trophy fish. "Wa'n't much keeping him together," he said. "We might can get all his scrawny limbs into one bag. No use wasting them."

Purvis slipped the leg into the bag and went back to work. Martha watched in silence, admiring the astounding economy with which he executed his task. He pressed in the blade and ringed the joints without ever removing his hand from the knife. A deft twist extracted the ball joint from its socket. The flesh on both sides of each split was flat and even, like a grocery store ham. Looking at the table, Martha was disappointed to see only a few purple drops of blood, not the pool she'd expected.

Purvis carved the final arm from the shoulder and dropped it into the bag.

"You do that pretty well," Martha said. "Focused."

"My old man told me there's two kinds of tools," Purvis said. "Sharp and blunt. 'Decide which one you're going to be, son,' he said." Purvis rubbed his thumb along the edge of the knife. "I reckon I'm mostly a blunt tool, but sometimes I can sharpen up. Ockham the Razor."

"What the hell are you talking about?"

"This philosopher, Ockham the Razor, said cut out what you don't need, and that'll make things truer," said Purvis. "My cousin that teaches at the college told me all about him. The old boy lived thousands of years ago, like that other one my cousin told me said a whole lot of smart stuff, Aristotle. I don't know if they ever come across each other, but that would've been some wicked shit. Godamighty! I bet they could've got into it big time."

"This Ockham... what did you say?"

"The Razor."

"Yeah, Ockham the Razor. He said get rid of dead weight, eh?" Martha asked.

"Yeah, dead weight, except this old monk I took propane to at the monk place said something about parsi, parsi money, maybe, and don't multiply something beyond..." Purvis looked up and squinted his eyes, as if trying to focus on an insect upon the ceiling. He tapped the hooked tip of the knife against his lip. "Hell, I can't recall what it was beyond. I just know what my cousin—you remember him, Legare?—told me."

"Focus, Purvis. What about the head?"

"Whose head?"

"Armey's fucking head!" Martha yelled. She laced her fingers behind her neck, arched her back, and blew a long gust of air at the ceiling. "Let's finish up and get out of here. Now, are you going to cut off his head?"

Purvis thought he saw a shudder ran through Martha's breasts. He thought of how his Uncle

Stafford's gobbler would spread his tail and shake when you got close to the turkey pen. A ripple would run through the bird, and its raised feathers would whir like a lawnmower cranking. All night Martha's movements, her facial expressions, her stance, seemed to Purvis to be signs she was throwing at him. The signs were getting deeper—arms around her head, limbs in a bag at her feet—and he needed more training in reading them. Armey had all those books at his house and probably knew about how to read symbols. But there he lay, deader than Aristotle and not whole.

"Purvis, focus again on what you're doing," said Martha.

"What you're doing."

"Goddamn it, just give me it," Martha said. She stepped toward Purvis and took his knife. She put her hand to Armey's chin and tilted his head. The throat offered itself up, the larynx as round as a hickory nut. "I should have done this fifteen years ago," she said as she pushed the blade into the far side two inches below the point of the jaw. It passed through the larynx and out the near side to *ping* against the table. She retraced the slice, deeper, through tissue, clearing the neck bone. She stabbed the point into Armey's chest as if standing it in a wheel of hoop cheese in a country store, and then, laying one hand upon his forehead and sliding the other to the base of the skull, jerked hard, separating the vertebrae. With one more pass of the knife, the head left the body. Blood leaked from both sides of the neck, collecting into an indigo circle the size of snuff can.

"That's better," Martha said.

Purvis marveled at the entire performance, his heart racing like an engine. His father was right, he realized, about how carving can bring people closer. Martha must know it, too, or why else would she have taken the knife and cut? It was more, though, than just something that needed doing together—it was a symboling dance. Her arms and legs and ass and tongue and pistol could talk a book, and she played Purvis's knife like a mandolin. He wanted to speak back to her in symbols, but maybe it didn't work that way. In a love like theirs, maybe one person gives the symbols and the other receives. The one who receives has to be ready every moment to catch them, like flickering lightning bugs.

"Open the bag." Martha held Armey's head, upside-down in one hand, by the bottom jaw, her fingers hooking behind the teeth. The image was spectacular, and Purvis thought he would cry. Martha looked like an armored warrior woman goddess from way back in Rome or Egypt who had just killed a sea monster and made the waters safe again. She started to place the head into the garbage bag, but Purvis reached down and grabbed a new one.

"I reckon it deserves its own bag," he said. Martha dropped it in, and Purvis tied the drawstrings. He rubbed his hands around the bag, as if guessing its contents.

"Here," Martha said, handing Purvis his knife. "You can have it back now."

"I think it's sharper than ever." He wiped it on the apron and slid it into his pocket.

They put the torso into another bag and loaded the dismembered body into the back of the truck, next to Larson, still asleep. The sky, clear now, was full of stars, navigational signs for those who could read them.

* * *

"You know what the hell time it is?" DeWayne said, standing in his doorway in just his underwear. "I got to drag my ass up in a couple of hours."

"You got to go with us to the hash plant," Purvis said. "I got something in the back of your truck we got to dispose."

"Fuck that. I'll take it tomorrow."

"It's got to be now."

"What the hell for?"

"Armey."

"How you mean for Armey? You said he was..." Then DeWayne spotted one of the bags in the back of the truck. He dropped his head and rubbed his face with both hands. "I ain't believing. Jesus on a pine plank. A human man body. This ain't real."

"What's real is the FBI on it," said Purvis. "Martha said they were asking all kind of questions about me—"

"That crazy bitch out there in my truck? She's hauled you into some crucial shit and now you hauling me into it."

"You don't know how it is." Purvis wiped his eyes and began to talk fast. "It's all coming at me like needles of light and me trying to catch them, but they stick to me, pulling me into a drowning place—"

"What's coming at you?"

"Her symbols, and then it tastes like metal, like lead or copper, just when my head goes under. But then she's like the boat for me, and her arms fanning out like a feeler gauge and shining in her symboling dance, and I'm trying to read it, trying to read it all," said Purvis. "I got to do it and then do this other thing for her, and we'll fly off or like up a beanstalk, and then things'll go away from me and from her and me just a redneck sapsucker, and you don't know a shit I'm talking about but you got to help or I'll—"

"I knew I shouldn't've let you borrow my truck."

"I gassed it up."

"Not enough." DeWayne exhaled a heavy blast and turned to the side. "A punch."

"Bullshit."

"Just one punch and I'll get dressed and drive the Isuzu and you two follow me in the propane truck. He covered up?"

"Three bags."

"Baby Jesus in a biscuit. You cut the son of a bitch up?"

"Carved."

DeWayne held his fists in a boxing stance. "I don't know who's working graveyard shift tonight. I'll pull in and take care of it while y'all wait out front. Got it?" He dipped his right shoulder and pantomimed an uppercut. "Now, one punch."

"Just not on my lip where them wasps bit it. They got my ear, too, and—"

The fist connected to Purvis's wasp-stung ear, spurting blood and puss out onto his neck and DeWayne's knuckles. "Screw a guinea," Purvis said, choking a little. "I been trying to pop that bad boy all day."

"Does it hurt?" Martha asked. "Grown men punching each other."

"Not much," Purvis said. "It's just a brother thing. We been doing that since we was kids. I wish he'd've busted my goddamn nose and taken the edge off this hash stink. Or maybe if I had another swallow of that purple jesus, that would dead it out." He sat up high in the seat, peering toward the rendering plant's front door. "He's coming out finally."

DeWayne crossed the parking lot into the shadows, where they sat in the propane truck. "He's a new guy," DeWayne said through Purvis's window. "Dude named Winky. Worried about he'll lose his job. Somehow we hadn't crossed shifts so he don't know me."

"What's for him to get in trouble for?" Purvis asked. "What'd you tell him it was?"

"I said you were this fellow I know that let a couple his daddy's hogs die he was in charge of and want to make it look like the hogs broke through the fence. He gets the fidgets and starts to sweating and carrying on about 'I got to keep account of every time the grinder runs' and 'I don't need suspicion.' And I say, 'Goddog, I'll just load them in and they gone, we do it all the time,' and he says, 'I don't know who *we* is but this old boy ain't one of *we*' and I say—"

"How much does he want?" Martha asked.

"Fifty dollars," said DeWayne.

"Shit on *we*," Purvis said.

"Here," Martha said. She took a roll of bills from her pocket and handed DeWayne a twenty. "Tell him take it or leave it." DeWayne went back inside.

"What if he don't take it?" Purvis asked.

"Let's just see."

In a few seconds, DeWayne and Winky emerged. Climbing into the Isuzu, Winky drove around the back of the building, while DeWayne came to the propane truck.

"He said he's got do it hisself," said DeWayne.

"Why you not back there with him?" Purvis asked.

"Ain't nothing to it," said DeWayne. "Just put the shit in the front-end loader, drop it into the grinder, and it eats it up bones and all. Ain't like we're cooking and separating like a normal job."

140

"What the fuck?" cried Winky, running around the corner of the building. "There's a man in there!"

"Godamighty!" said Purvis as he and Martha jumped from the truck. "He must've opened them damn bags!" The three ran to the building.

"What you trying to do to me?" Winky yelled. "Twenty dollars my ripe ass!"

Winky led them inside. And there, eight feet off the ground, in the pan of the front-end loader, Larson sat up, the tarp loosened around his chest, his arms in the air. "I'm flying! I'm flying!" he said.

"Wrong bag," said Purvis. "I reckon you tell that ain't no hog. That's right there's a retard."

"Get him down!" Martha yelled.

DeWayne climbed into the loader and lowered the pan.

"I'm falling! Woo hee!" Larson yelled.

Unwrapping the rest of the tarp from Larson, Purvis and Martha sat him onto the tailgate. Purvis put the garbage bags into the loader, and DeWayne drove it into the building. Winky, gasping, leaned against the truck fender.

"Take a squirt of this," said Purvis, offering his albuterol inhaler. "I got the asthma and get the wheezes all the time."

Winky took a puff. "Hate this damn job. Out here all night. Smells like a mountain of assholes. And me with a bad heart."

"We all got a bad heart," Purvis said. He tapped his cigarette pack. Out popped a joint. "This might help some."

"I believe it will," Winky said, lighting up.

"Way high," Larson said. "Fly me again way high, woo, and give me a suck on that little something the gas man won't give me I asked him for."

"Hush, sweetie," Martha said.

DeWayne returned. "Hogs all took care of. Let's head out. Sorry we gave you such a scare, Winky."

"Hogs hell," Winky said. "What y'all had in them bags?"

"Like you said," Purvis said, "a man." He slapped Winky's back.

Winky coughed, and slowly released smoke through his nose. "Twenty dollars my ripe ass."

Purvis looked out the propane truck window. "I know some constellation names," he said. "Yonder's the Big Dipper, which is pretty easy, but did you know its real name is something like Ursa maker and is Roman or Egyptian or some shit what means the Big Bear? The two stars at the front edge of the pot point at the Little Dipper, what's really called the Little Bear, and the tip of its handle is the North Star." He sighted along his arm like a rifle, his other hand on the wheel. "That's what everybody uses to navigate. Even sailors back in like Bible days followed them same ones. Signs. We all need signs." Purvis pressed his hand against the ear Dewayne had punched. "I don't see them right now, but there's a line of three that lots of dumbasses think's a dipper, but it's Orion the Hunter. He's my favorite, but he must be down below the trees now. The three is his magic belt, and with a sword hanging offen it. There's a half circle up above, that's his bow he hunts with. Plenty animals up there for him to shoot at—a lion, a bull, a goose. Wait, not goose. What they call that other big stretch-neck duck kind of bird?

"Swan?"

"Yeah, swan. I don't believe I ever seen one. I wonder if they're good eating? Them big old things could feed a bunch of people. I know people what eats about anything. Possum, snake, cooter. I've heard, now I don't know it to be a fact, but I've heard that Chinamen'll eat dog. I've eat possum a couple of times, and I'd eat snake if I knowed the poison was washed out, but I ain't about to eat no damn dog. They stink."

"Stink!" Larson yelled. He jumped up from where he was curled in the back to lean over the truck console between Purvis and Martha. "Stink truck! Gas truck man got a stink truck!"

"Hush, Larson," Martha said. "Purvis, you're especially talkative tonight."

"I am? I reckon I *am* a little nervous." He lit two cigarettes and gave one to Martha. "I wish I hadn't given that Winky guy my last doob."

"It was the sharp thing to do," said Martha. "Besides, you're tired."

"Sharp." He smiled for a second, then ground his jaw and wrinkled his brow. He pinched the bridge of his nose. "I know what to do, think I do, but it's just all here, all around, coming at me."

"What is?"

"All of it, and me in the midst, just got to go, but nothing to go on or where."

"I might have something to go on," said Martha. "Stop here so we won't wake Mother."

Purvis stopped and cut off the truck in front of the cattle guard. "You do, I mean, you are. Something to go on," he said. "Like I said, I'm a sharp tool some of the time, but mostly a blunt one, good for bamming, not for clear-seeing."

"Where we at?" Larson asked. "Aunt Ruthie's and you live here too house, and I'm staying. Spending on a pallet, not in a truck for sleeping no more."

"Hush, Larson," Martha said. "Purvis, I told you about Florida."

"Jacaranda." He looked into Martha's face. The features began to shift across her face in a wave. Another sign. "Jacaranda."

"Yes. We'll see Jacarandas and dolphins and pelicans and lots and lots of orange trees. Oranges sweeter than honey. I'll take care of us down there, Purvis. You and me and the Jacarandas."

"Jacky Randy," Larson said. "You Jacky Randy."

Purvis jerked his head around and growled at Larson, "Don't say that."

Larson giggled and poked Purvis in the shoulder. "Jacky Randy! Your name, the gas truck man, Jacky Randy!"

Martha opened the door. "Pick me up at the flower shop tomorrow at five," she said. "Let's go, Larson."

Grunting, Larson tried to climb over the console. He slipped and fell to his stomach, his heel snapping up to kick Purvis in the ear.

"Goddammit!" Purvis rubbed his ear. "Now I got two sore ears!"

Martha helped Larson crawl from the cab. He placed his foot onto the cattle guard and balked. "I can't walk that no ground but holes to the ditch and fall in it."

Martha nudged him. "You can do it."

"I'm falling!" Larson hollered.

Then Purvis came out of the truck and, in one smooth motion, swept Larson up, carrying him across the metal pipes.

"I'm flying!" Larson said.

"Everybody needs toting sometimes," Martha said.

"Some needs toting all the time," said Purvis.

"The Art of Carving" is excerpted from *Purple Jesus*, Bancroft Press, 2010.

_____ Child(ren) Left Behind
Esther G. Belin

Complete the following sentence then support your answer with evidence:

_____ saw Chief Joseph today while looking at _____

While crawling into the oxygen deprived space. I only had a second to look. I only had time to...

_____
_____
_____

Here is my list:
1. The white hen.
2. Walking forward (_Soli Deo Gloria_).
3. The war we are playing is called_____.
4. The Issei woman, a trickster holding blossoms of broken English.
5. You say, "Tell me." I repeat the Declaration of Independence.
6. The barely visible target reveals/revels/wrestles with printed text.
7. My beach stretches a thousand miles and I can see the mating whales.
8. Chief_____ was laughing in between the photo shoot; he was sitting atop a horse.
9. That damn smile led to that amazing kiss...

Create a line graph, then breathe air into the blow up person you create:

Sunset Beach	1986	Abiqui
1994	battlefield	green curry
Crow Fair	river	white buffalo
Oklahoma	dentalium shells	New Year's Eve
beans and frybread	Indian corn	red chile

On War
Esther G. Belin

Us   Them
_____

who are they?

                        that are occupying the land we

we never
you always
discovered

                                     conquered

Us
_____

The morning of our death we were prepared
Salvia chewed into the vision shared

The sinew threaded through the parchment signed
Stacked into neat piles, a boundary line

The war cries billow the mound builder's spine
Layers of hot flesh with marrow entwined

The lightning-tipped rainbow scented like dust
A taste full as the reflection of us

                                        Them
_____

We are eager to explore and see what adventures
could benefit us I believe in steadfastness in this
journey I believe in Moby Dick I believe in shooting
stars I believe in the Almighty God that created the
friction underneath our footprint I believe in the path
furrowed in the ridges of each thumbprint I believe in
the union between two continents

147

Public Records 1831
Esther G. Belin

1. Chief Justice John Marshall created our mythic image: "domestic dependent nations."
2. The basic principle of modern federal Indian Policy: small insertions of the "Doctrine of Discovery" serum, prescribed during each new fiscal year. Side effects from long term use: Genocide.
3. Indian Health Service: "How long has your Indian blood been killing you?"
4. The secretary took his words. They are now Public Record:

the eager wait to read and write in solaced tunnels,
    under covers, on side of bridges
the hungry are eager to swallow, fluid, solid, both at
    the same time

they swallow
swill
down
small packages like
a lover's tongue like
a stirring pot
like a long time after
death has occurred
the record
records

recordings like
stained linen parchment
cataloguing like
the rhythmic swinging of limbs
the nestling of the unborn
the tidal pull, saturating the tender lining
between
the scratchy turning of
histories

the mechanical swagger like
the latest trading post novel
post-
indian
postage
like a forever stamp
Aszdaan Tlogi nishli
I am and I lick the corners
of the I am that I am today
stuffed neatly into a medical bill
oh
we are out of _____ again
again
the prescribed medication
the pharmacist asks for my signature
as public record
again

Sending the Letter Never Sent
Esther G. Belin

...all I can do is moan.
 And, if I didn't tell you,
 I would be angry at you for not listening,
 blaming you for what I haven't spoken.
 —David Mura

And wail
my anger trapped in my own brain cells
the thought behind the unspoken
is more than
what rolls off the tongue

From
those whose tongue is only in the first ceremony
the many ceremonies to follow
voice the unspoken

And those who speak
get plump from decorated shells of modernism

My own shame catches
as my brain shouts at itself
voice cracked and sore

You will not

Listen, I know I told you it before
yea, yeah, Indians have their land stolen
yeah, yeah, it sucks we use them as mascots
yeah, yeah, tell me something new

I want to know why
skins drink so much
call themselves Indians

There's no real reason to complain
we're still around
breeds mostly
blending cultures generic
proud to be made in America
living off the fruits of its land
BIA
CIA
USA

Just say no
Just say it's a long story
my mind is telling
not for just one sitting
hundreds of winter evenings
to tell all these stories
No instant just add water
this is telepathic

Long ago
we believed the same
and difference only made our faith stronger.

"Sending the Letter Never Sent" reprinted from "From the Belly of My Beauty" (c) Esther Belin, University of Arizona Press, 1999. Used by permission.

Separation
Esther G. Belin

mile post 54
hwy 491
dirt road 192
1 1/4 miles west

there you should find a house
with a red metal roof
the house
that contains
my Navajo Education

lesson 38
not a bar
not a casino
not a hogan
it all began in a car
the kids are restless
tired of being confined to this holding tank
and this time it is cold
there is early snow calculated from the dark cloudy
mountains
the kids are restless
tired of telling jokes
tired of playing "I Spy"
tired of tribal radio

assignment 38
1. diagram the separation
2. write a poem about the language not spoken
3. rearrange lines in symbolic order

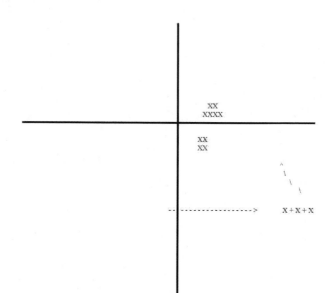

assignment 39
1. diagram the separation
2. write a poem about the language not spoken
3. rearrange lines in symbolic order

27 Trap
Michael Gills

The summer before my senior year, when I'd not yet understood that nobody makes it out of Lonoke alive, one of our assistant football coaches was fired for an incident that indirectly involved me and for which he held a grudge. Coach Webb, I'll call him, was rehired by our cross state nemesis, Bauxite, where he fabricated a letter to the varsity football team and signed my name to it. The letter was vile—it said things.

We'd ripped their asses the year before, the Bulldogs. A black and white from the Saturday morning *Gazette* had flashed my number: *HARVELL HOPS DOGS,* the headline said. It'd been their Homecoming, all the chiffon-gowned queens decked out on a glittery float, glass stones shining in their tiaras. Near the end, the Bulldog band played "Smoke on the Water" and one of the Maids of Honor was crying, her mascara dripping off her chin staining her pink dress. I imagined her slow dancing with a whipped linebacker, whispering, "It's okay, baby. Really, it doesn't matter. It's nothing," and knowing in her heart she didn't mean it, that this night would follow her for the rest of her life.

What I'm saying is it wasn't pretty. And on the bus ride home a red-eyed opossum ran onto the highway and the big tires thumped him over, no joy in that.

* * *

That spring after we crushed Bauxite, Curtis LeRoy, our inside linebacker—he ran with these kids who called themselves *don't give a damners*, sort of a Klan for high schoolers—had solicited four of us to help Coach Webb move into a mobile home out on Highway 5. After, Coach'd made milkshakes and cheese dip, set up his entertainment center and shown a porn movie. I'd never seen anything like it, and I remember thinking *whoa*. But I watched, all the same. Head Coach Humphries somehow got wind of it and questioned each of us at some length about exactly what had happened.

Coach Webb's contract wasn't renewed for the next year.

I never thought twice about it until the night of our last senior game, when the Bulldogs trotted onto the field for warmups wearing with *KILL #45*, or *#45 IS DEAD* writ all over their uniforms and armpads and helmets. The mascot bulldog dragged a dummy with a noose around its neck, wearing what I swear to god was my jersey from last year—the same rip in the left shoulder, the curve of the five sloughing off. This was November, right before Thanksgiving and the holiday deer hunt. My girlfriend's father, Reese Curly, ran Century 21 Real Estate in Lonoke, and he'd given me a job hauling around and setting FOR SALE signs, then painting them purple—which means *posted* if you're in Arkansas and can't read. Otherwise deer hunters would shoot them full of holes with high-powered rifles. They were heavy fuckers—it took a three-foot hole dug with posthole diggers to hold one of those mothers, but he paid cash, and it kept me around his house on weekends which was fine by me.

Toni was five-ten, a brown-eyed beauty and genius who'd won Miss Jackrabbit for performing a soliloquy from *Hamlet*. She could make herself cry and laugh and be confused and clear-headed all at once, and I'd witnessed her belch "Yellow Rose of Texas" after a trayful of her daddy's mixed drinks. She'd choreographed this cheer with a lot of hips and my name in it that the squad was to try out that night. Mr. Curley was having a party for us all after the game and there'd be liquor, forbidden by county blue laws, and therefore what we desired most on this earth, to crush Bauxite Bulldogs and get wonderfully snockered with the sweet Jackrabbit cheer squad.

During warm ups, Cummings, the Bulldog tailback, caught me on the fifty, about to turn back toward home goal after a practice sweep. We'd run track against each other, those lazy spring meets when there'd be six hours between prelims and finals, enough time to get to know your opponents, share a bucket of chicken. "You write that letter, Harvell?"

"What letter?"

He reached up under his shoulder pads, pulled out a piece of paper, unfolded it and passed it to me. "Says it's from you, but some of us ain't sure."

The stadium lights got bright. Up in the stands, there was my mother and sisters filing into their seats. The Curleys were there opposite Curtis LeRoy's grizzled people. Walking around the cinder track, Bulldog parents—a whole slew of them. The scrawled words were not my hand at all, but familiar. Coach Humphries screamed just as I got to the worst of it.

"Here," I said. "I never wrote that." Taylor and I met the Bulldog captains at the fifty for the flip. Cummings walked out with number fifty, the Bulldog noseman, *MURDER #45* magic-markered across his jersey mesh. Over on the guest sideline, there was Coach Webb, this serene look on his face. He saw me see him.

Taylor called tails and won. We shook the bulldog

hands, only the noseman had something in his that bit right into my palm. He said, "You're dead."

"Wasn't me wrote that letter."

The refs led us to our respective sides of the field, made the sign for Jackrabbits receiving, Bulldogs kicking.

"Sure," he said and buckled his chin strap, the T-guard facemask gashed in a few places and maybe fifty stickers for big hits all around the ear holes. He lifted the elastic of a heavy arm pad and there shone the silver hilt of a Buck knife.

"I swear," I said, blood leaking out of my right fist.

Game Day before school, Lonoke First Baptist held a pancake breakfast in Family Hall, where Brother Stag Burnett introduced whichever one of us had been chosen to speak. That week it was Aubrey, our quarterback, a wiry blond kid whose father was military. He'd been at Coach Webb's that day, too. Offense had worked up a new play for the Bulldogs, a counter-trap with a right guard crackback. It'll kill 'em, Coach had said after we ran the play against meat-squad D. So after Brother Stag's introduction, Aubrey mumbled something about daily walking with Jesus who was Jackrabbit to the bone, we grazed on sugar-dusted pancakes and went over the play with pads of butter for the defense.

The 27 Trap is built on sudden, ferocious duplicity. We ran out of the *I*, a fullback and tailback with a slot and tight-end to the strong side, which usually meant the direction of the play, only that was pure feint with the 27. A counter sets all the weight and motion toward a fake strong side—so for the 27, a quick hitter, when the ball is snapped everyone goes right except for the pulling guard who throws a wicked crackback block on the noseman, who would have lined up in the seven hole, and—if he was real unlucky—was about to stunt. Aubrey would take the snap, spin right to the strong side just as the fullback blasted through the eight hole to take out the middle linebacker. I'd blast right, then cut hard behind the guard's crackback.

Aubrey lined up three pads of butter as linebackers. "Black 27," he said, and ran his butter knife through the eight hole, slapped the hunks of butter clean to the end of our table where Brother Staggs was oogling a girl basketball player.

"Harvell scores," he shouted.

The whole length of the First Baptist Jackrabbit Pancake Breakfast table stared at us and there was a spattering of applause. Even Brother Stag brought his hands out from under the table, and the glazed-eyed basketball girl looked up too.

"*Go Jackrabbits*," somebody said. "*Pound the dogs!*"

Said another, "*Amen.*"

Our first play from scrimmage was the Trap. The bulldog kick had skipped out at the thirty, the wideouts from the kickoff team sprinting up screaming something about *45's dead* and *kill fucker boy,* and *you don't talk about my mama*, something like that. A bugle sounded, and I could hear the cheerleaders chant, Toni Curley out there with her thighs new-shaved.

Curtis LeRoy had stepped in at fullback to throw the lead block in a sweep right—the play that was *supposed* to start our drive.

"Sweep right, 92," Aubrey said into the bent over huddle. "On two." We lined up strong right. Aubrey screamed, "Blue, thirty-two, thirty-two."

Only number 50 hopped into the seven-hole gap. He hollered *Tango Loco,* Bulldog code for a stunt. I thought about the Buck knife, the old stories about players getting back-stabbed in the pile. It happened. A few years back, somebody bit the tip end off DeWanye Pemberton's little finger. "*Black 27. Black 27.*" Aubrey'd read the stunt, screamed the changed play right, then left. On snap, our entire motion started right, and the D leaned with us. One step into his blitz, number 50 got blind-sided by Taylor, our pulling guard, a wicked crackback. I took the handoff right, cut left and heard the crunch of vertebra, the pitiful cry. Bauxite's safety didn't have a chance, the angle was all mine. Curtis LeRoy galloped off in the flats. It was a seventy-yard run, and I high-stepped across the goal line. Blood pumped through me, the breath steaming through my mask. I listened for my name over the loudspeaker, but when I turned back, the stadium was stunned silent.

"You *faggot.*" Curtis LeRoy spat through his mask.

The band shut down. A fire truck squalled in the distance. It rolled around the cinder track to the thirty, and out came two volunteer firemen with a stretcher. It took a long time. People held their piss. No one moved or talked or walked for a popcorn at the concession stand. They strapped number 50, the boy who'd just been paralyzed from the neck down for life, secured his head. And when they carried him off, the crowd clapped some. We beat the bulldogs 21- 7, but nobody's heart was in it. Not after that.

"Good game," Cummings said after, as we filed past each other and shook at midfield.

I said, "Sorry."

"It's all fucked up," he said and looked at his

shoes.

A few of the other players shook my hand. "You still a slippery one," Coach Webb said out of nowhere. We met eyes—just for a second. Then he walked off the cinder track and I never saw him again.

One of the shower heads in the locker room had stuck on, so steam rolled out the open door while a manager cut athletic tape off my ankles. I pulled jeans on at my locker, ran a comb through my hair. Curtis LeRoy, still in his pads, sat against a wall. He glared then covered his eyes. I think he was crying. He'd called me *faggot*, the word in the fake letter that had so riled the Bulldogs. We'd once been friends—before he became a *damner.* Maybe he was replaying in his head, the trap that scathed its way into our hearts and minds in the days and months and years to come.

This was in the day when adults serving liquor to underage drinkers was not so frowned upon as it is today, or that's how it seems to me now. I first met Reese Curley at a brisk fall after game party when cider spliced with bourbon steamed in mugs stirred with cinnamon sticks, and there was a fire on, and he was chalking up a cue stick and sinking balls on the billiards table in their den. They lived on a gentle hill that overlooked the country club far in the distance, a place where people with money bought forty acres of farm land and built these huge ranch houses with big swimming pools and triple car garages with flagstone driveways that lay out sleek and shining for a couple hundred yards to the main road, where there was a gate that opened electronically. As a Century 21 realtor, he'd somehow swung the house—a real monster with tons of cedar and stone, copper gutters and a shake shingle roof that shone on the hillside which that let grow natural. Inside were wide, airy rooms, with big windows so the natural light shone of the soft colors and sweet-new carpet that adjoined to Italian tile and maple. It was the nicest home I'd ever seen, a real trophy, especially for Lonoke, where my own people still rented, and the suburbs hadn't really dug in yet so most lived in run down farm houses and ramblers and decrepit Victorians. They'd moved up from North Little Rock, Reese and Alana, so people didn't trust them I don't guess, with their beauty queen daughter who quoted Shakespeare and spoke French.

His specialty, Reese's, was the Harvey Wallbanger, a drink named for a man who was supposed to have banged his head against a wall after having a snoot full. That night, from his post behind the wet bar in the den, he mixed them by the trayful, iced rocks glasses concocted to the rim with the vodka, o.j., and Galliano liquor, garnished with bright maraschino cherries, and Alana was playing through her old swing 45s. A fire had been set in the big stone hearth and hors d'oeuvres were laid out on a pale blue sheet draped over the pool table, five different cheeses and stuffed mushrooms, olives skewered through with slivers of smoked oyster and garlic, pickled okra, a summer sausage and salami platter, cheese dip and guacamole and homemade salsa, a whole platter of pizza wedges—the whole nine yards. Toni had met me outside the fieldhouse, and we'd driven up together, her in the purple cheer skirt and me smelling of soap and cheap shampoo. She'd punched the code at the big front gate, and Reese had come over the speaker. "Well you two have taken your time," he said, and it sounded like a party inside. "Do I need to consult with Maggie?"

Maggie was Reese's .30-ought six, and he'd written

my name with a felt marker on one silver-tip cartridge the night of Junior Prom. "Just so you know," he'd said, though Toni'd laughed, said, "You wouldn't dare."

"Well here we are, Daddy," Toni said, and we drove up the long, dark drive, got out, and she led me inside by the hand that the paralyzed Bulldog had shook, the blood dry now.

Nearly the whole starting offense showed up—with each arrival, the voices came over an invisible speaker, and Reese spoke into a microphone, that happy note as he pushed the button that unlocked the front gate. Adults filtered in too: Dewey Fawcett and his wife, the Utleys, Mr. and Mrs. Self and a woman in a see-through black skirt who made change at Suds and Duds, Mr. Curley's laundromat.

Toni wore my letter jacket, 45 in big white numbers on the left shoulder. The lights were low and the music soft, the fire popped now and again, and the drink trays came and came again. One Harvey Wallbanger tastes sweet and warm, and the second goes down like honey-laced medicine, and the third hooks up with the thing you'd most like to be in life, and transforms you into exactly that. After three, who gives a flying fuck.

I remember running a few plays with a NERF football, Reese lining up in the fallen linebacker slot. How we looked at each other during the trap, and I thought that it must be bad luck.

Leah joined Toni and the cheerleaders, shaking her kinky red hair, her voice harmonizing with theirs. They performed a boozy "Are You Satisfied," with grunts and hip thrusts right on the money, then Toni made the call for the cheer she'd come up with for *me—Harvell, out of your shell, ring the bell, give 'em hell,* something like that. They'd lined up like a chorus

163

line, right legs cocked, hands on hips. We were all happy by then, and somebody'd broken out eggs and slab bacon, I could smell it frying.

"*Harvell*," came the voice over the staticky speaker. "*Send out faggot.*"

They'd just finished "Funky on our Feet," so the room was quiet and Curtis LeRoy's surly voice drawled again—"Send Harvell to the gate."

Outside the huge front window, the *damners* had erected one of Reese's For Sale signs. It burst into orange flame right in front of our faces. "Dear God," Ms. Curley said.

"*Send us your pussy,*" LeRoy said.

Reese left the room, returned with Maggie, the scoped .30-ought-six which he shouldered, eye-balling them through the 3 x 9 wide-lens. He off-clicked the safety. The woman in the see-through dress said, "*No, no, no, no, no.*"

Once Curtis had been run over by a car out on Mountain Springs Road, had his jaws wired shut, and I took him a crockpot of bean soup. His daddy owned County Line Liquor, everybody'd heard the stories.

"*Ain't got no truck with you Curleys. Send fucker-boy.*"

Toni walked to the bar, picked up the microphone, and in the same movie-star voice she'd one day use to accept the Miss America crown, said, "*Mayonnaise.*" The long *a* and *o* linked musically in her throat.

There was this white-hot light in her eyes, the For Sale sign burning and twinkling there in her pupils. "*Mayonnaise,*" she said again. She looked at the mike and said the odd word a third time—who knew why?

I smelled gun oil, and pictured the world of hurt a big deer rifle like that could do to a seventeen-year-old. I wondered how much light would shine through a ribcage with a hole the size of a bucket lid blown through it.

All was quiet.

Then LeRoy's taillights flared, his engine turned over. The pickup moved a few feet and stopped. Then the truck pulled away slowly, hit the road and disappeared. The sign burned out and the sun came up. We went through the scrambled eggs, devoured bacon and buttered toast, and it was just a November Saturday. I never much talked to Curtis LeRoy again after that—he bleeped off my radar. Senior year rocketed past, and before I knew it I was working a concrete crew, saving money for college, the first Harvell to ever darken the door. That night was pretty much the end of me and Toni Curley, too. A few years later, she won Miss Arkansas, and then Miss U.S.A., where she wore a pixieish haircut, and was asked exactly what people did on Saturday nights in Lonoke. She played the hick and knocked their socks off. I remember watching, the gleam in her eyes—the same way she'd looked when she humiliated Curtis LeRoy, or when she delivered a monologue or kissed you on the lips. She was fourth runner-up in Ms. Universe, and Wayne Newton proposed to her, bought Reese and Leah a German Shepherd and put them up in the Bellagio on the Las Vegas strip for a month. She moved away from Lonoke and Arkansas forever, just like me. Last I heard, Reese had died—the big C—and his death had somehow transformed her. She'd become sort of a famous healer and spiritual coach, a picture of her flowing hair and glittery brown eyes on a self-help book, how she'd made the journey through the valley of the shadow of death, and survived, and she could teach you how to do the same.

I haven't talked to her since she got real big, but I did give her a ride to the University after she won Miss Arkansas. It was fall and we'd driven the pig trail, the tree's blazing and that crisp nip in the air, like when we'd all burst through the paper jackrabbit, and our mothers would cry and remember us that way. My car had overheated way out in the country and I'd had to steal a bucket from a fall down barn a fill it with water from the spigot of a stranger's house. People out here owned guns, for Jesus sake, that's what she said, laughing at the spectacle we made. Kicked back in the bucket seats, we waited for the engine light to go off. Her hair smelled good. "What happened to that kid who broke his neck? The one with kill 45 on his jersey?"

"They all had kill 45 on their jerseys," I said.

"Remember?"

"Yea."

"That night. I knew I'd leave Lonoke and never go back."

Steam hissed from the uncapped radiator, and her voice was silky—a made for radio voice. She was looking at herself in the sideview. "*Mayonnaise?*" I asked. What was that about?"

She looked at me through tiger slit eyes, and I saw it register. "I can't go home," she said. "Not ever."

"Why?"

Tears came then—and I remembered how she'd learned to make herself cry at will, how it had been to taste her liquory breath by the fire. How she could belch "Yellow Heart of Texas." She smiled, said, "Let's get out of here, Joe."

The thermostat in my Cutlass was bad, and I didn't know it, but there was water in the oil—the block was cracked. My car had maybe a hundred miles left in it, tops. I was twenty-one, and in the seat next to me sat Miss Arkansas, soon to be Miss U.SA.. Why not hit the road, keep on running? I said, "Sure, Toni," and got out to steal another bucketful of well water from

166

the sucked up farmhouse. "Soon as this car's alright. We're getting the hell out."

When I dropped her off in front of Pomfret Hall, she smiled and waved and looked embarrassed. Her eyes got big and glowed for a second, the way the sky does in the morning just before day comes.

Some stories sneak up on you down the road.

Last June, my wife, daughter and I made the drive across the Rocky Mountains, down through Illinois and Missouri to the black-dirt delta land of my people. We ate barbecue sandwiches outside Fayetteville, hit the pig trail and drove past the very piece of earth where I'd once broken down. So long out west, I wanted to leap from my car and hug anyone of color, and my heart lifted with the first cropdusters, flying eights over fields of milo and soy. Close to Lonoke, a funeral party drove by with a state trooper out in front with his lights swirling. We pulled off on a stretch that just so happened to be next to a cotton field and my daughter whooped with joy. She got out of the car, ran up a row, picked fistfuls and threw them up so they rained like Utah snowflakes in her golden hair. "Daddy," she cried through the open window. "I've read about this in books!"

This for plain-Jane cotton.

At the Jackrabbit class of 1979s thirtieth reunion, after suffering multiple playings of "Everybody Was Kung Fu Fighting" and "Born to Be Wild" and the entire flipping soundtrack of *Saturday Night Fever*, danced to by once lithe girls who now shook monumental rumps at bald classmates whose bellies swung like feed sacks over belt buckles, after the fish fry and banana pudding and iced tea and the mind numbing shock that I was not in the least out of place, that these were my kith and kin, even the few mellowed *damners* who'd shown up, Buzz Hawkins, our old defensive tackle and now Head Coach, invited us down to the new Jackrabbit fieldhouse in the north end zone, with its indoor playing field and air-conditioned film screening theater.

Though it was only June, the heat was on, and the wispy mirage clouds rose off asphalt all down the hill to the new stadium. I thought about Toni Curley, where she might be now, if she'd inherited Maggie, or Reese's inclination to get every last person standing dog drunk.

Inside was dark, cavernous—Hawkins hit a button that made this huge garage-like door come down on the half-field, and led us through metal doors.

"Just like the movies," Taylor said. "Where's the popcorn?"

Hawkins motioned us to the front, then took his place up at the controls. "I had them all *digitized* last spring. Check this."

Aubrey'd stayed trim—kept most of his hair. "Go Rabbits," he said. It was the same voice, not much different.

We took our seats, leaned back as the room faded to dark and it was quiet, and the food was heavy in my belly, and it would have been nice to go to sleep, just take a nippy-nap right there in the air-conditioned quiet, my wife and daughter safe back at the Day's Inn pool with the other alumni families, not a mile from where my nuts had dropped.

And there we were. In the vacuum quiet, the lot of us, seventeen-eighteen again, fleet and shining with the ghost light on our faces.

In slow-motion, I took Aubrey's pitch, cut hard toward the two hole as Taylor pulled right, leveled the corner, before the inside linebacker knocked me into the chains.

The film froze us. We sat stone still.

I could not have predicted this in a million years—like watching the future backwards.

Last came Bauxite, the kick-off followed by the 27 Trap. Hawkins let it roll. Aubrey checked off. We saw it coming down the pike, the violent crackback, the boy's neck snapping, my hard cut. The camera man just caught my high-step at the goal, Curtis LeRoy spitting that word, then focused on the horrified circle that gathered around the paralyzed boy. The moment when the ambulance door slammed, and the vehicle herky-jerky into the dark.

That was thirty years ago. Story was, LeRoy'd had a Purple Jesus party out at his house near Mountain Springs—just across the pasture from Coach Webb's trailer when things were still up in the air about his contract. It was a full moon, all these stoned sixteen, seventeen-year-old *damners* stumbling around in a field with purple circles around their mouths, a wood fire burning. Some drunk kid took his clothes off and pitched them in the fire, and soon everybody'd followed suit. Silly-kid stuff. Toni Curley'd been there—with Curtis—I'd find out too late to matter. A fistfight had broken out. This *damner* everyone called China Boy—his daddy ran the town funeral home—showed up with a jar of something like mayonnaise.

If you believe what they say, these kids smeared themselves with the stuff and did things that would turn your pee blue, unspeakable acts that not a single witness would ever discuss, except to say, "Just mention mayonnaise in front of any of them. See what happens."

Hell, they were just kids. So what? Like we used to say—*nobody was killed.*

**

Sudden, ferocious duplicity—the trap.

Hawkins brought the lights up again, and the four of us walked out onto Jackrabbit Stadium's new AstroTurf, hot and springy beneath our feet. Painted lines blazed, amongst block numbers and hash marks, the sound of a motorcycle driving old Honeysuckle Lane which still circled the field outside the far fence. The cinder track had been replaced with a hard red surface, and the scoreboard was this gigantic snarling jackrabbit with a barn-sized television screen built into it. It was something to see. Although there was no need to reenact anything ever again now, Hawkins had brought mesh-bag full of new-leather balls, and before I knew it we'd stripped off our street shoes and were running plays. Aubrey lobbed semi-wounded ducks at our flies and hooks, Taylor executing a pull for the 92 Sweep. Out west, I'd made a point of staying in passable shape—good enough to ski with my daughter, so the memory of having once possessed speed thrummed in my blood. My left arm tingled a little, pulse thumping in my neck. I saw him come walking toward us, through the gate at the far end of the field, onto the turf, our old middle linebacker with a motorcycle helmet in one hand.

"Boys," Curtis LeRoy said. "Long time, no see." His face was lined, and I thought of him in a field, dousing the sign with gasoline—how he must have looked through Reese Curley's high-powered rifle scope. "Can I play."

Aubrey pitched him a ball. "Sure, Curt. Hit me long."

Hawkins said, "I was wondering about you."

LeRoy threw a thirty-yard spiral to Aubrey's Cross. "We just got here from down south." He cleared his throat. "Dennis and me. He's back at the hotel. They's a pool party going on there."

LeRoy looked me in the eye. I said, "Dennis?"

"Yea," he said. "Ain't it the shits?"

Aubrey trotted back. We formed into the I, and got set. "Black twenty-seven. Black. Twenty-seven," he said.

The list of those who'd died from the Class of '79 had been read on stage in silence. Lisa Montclaire, whose raven hair fell on pale shoulders—I remember her in cutoffs dancing in the rain after a fish fry and how the world dazzled in her blue eyes. Ken Manti, our safety, who'd I'd gotten kicked out of Chemistry class with for saying the word "sever" to Mr. Tiney who was a Mormon, I've never known why about the *sever* part. Others. A whole slew of our teachers had passed. One Coach, Humphries. Each in turn, they smiled down on us from the screen in the gymnasium where I'd once slow-danced with Dayna Barger, a 10th grade homecoming maid, whose father had died and who smelled like oranges through a yellow dress.

I got out.

I tell my daughter, a sophomore now, those people you worry about liking you, the ones you anguish over, you won't care in the least about them down the road. In thirty, forty years—they'll be nobody to you. You won't remember ever having cared.

The past won't mean a goddamn thing at all.

Cross Dressing
Larry Fondation

I want to drink alone.

I admire the bartender's tits, large and low-slung.

I manage to have three bourbons before the intrusion.

An unshaven man sits beside me. Unkempt, he has a story.

The jukebox plays un-loud.

The guy starts talking: "We just smoked them."

I order another whiskey.

"I got to say, the raghead chick was fine. I'd never fucked a sand nigger before."

At the pool table, this girl has the kind of perfect ass that comes from sitting on a barstool—spread-wide and beautiful.

"You got to get some benefit from serving over there, don't you think?"

"Makes sense," I mumble.

The place is cash only. I check my wallet. I have plenty.

"We had to kill them after we fucked them, you know what I mean?"

I look at my drink.

The lights blink.

I take a notebook from my jacket pocket and I begin to write.

"Hey, you writing about me? I got some stories..."

Barstool chick is good at pool. She laughs and coughs. I imagine her speaking voice.

"You ever do a tour?" the scruffy man asks.

"No," I lie.

My girl was Kuwaiti, twelve years ago, a time of restraint.

"We had no choice," the guy says, drawing close to my face.

Big-breast bartender serves me another.

Five drinks in, I am still un-fucked up.

Shaggy-guy's breath stinks.

I get up to play pool.

Beard-boy stays at the bar. I don't think he can stand.

A scuffle starts at the pool table.

I failed to write my name on the chalkboard.

I have to wait to play.

I sit back down.

I want no more story.

I think of 8th Grade: "Arma virumque cano."

"We strangled them all," he says. "Minimizes evidence."

I do not speak.

"No trip up the river," he says.

At last it is my turn to play pool.

Barfly chick is my opponent.

"Bet?" she asks. Her voice is low and scratchy. Perfect.

"You take me home if I win?"

"Ha!"

The felt on the table is fucked up.

She wins handily anyway.

"Consolation?" I ask.

"What?" I wish she would talk more.

"Walk me to my car?"

"Are you serious?"

"Yes," I say.

I turn to look towards the bar.

Un-razored man narrates to another.
I leave the bar for good.
I look over my shoulder for the name of the place.
I am out of luck.
I talk to myself all the way home.
(Shit out of luck.
It's a prosody I'm looking for.
I can never end things.)

"Cross Dressing" appeared in the collection *Martyrs and Holymen* (Raw Dog Screaming Press; 2013).

Road Noise
Mark Turcotte

for the man who was my father,
and for the man who is my son

Election Day 1

As America was stirring from its usual slumber, I
stood on the ice-encrusted steps of the church at St.
Ann's Mission. It was Election Day 1992, a stark and
stormy North Dakota morning. Shivering in my too-
thin coat, cupping a match to another cigarette, I
watched the cars filled with mourners grind up the
slippery hill. Below me, the men were struggling with
the weight of the long gray box, their thick, brown
hands cracking open in the freezing air as they huffed
up the steps, shuffled past me, and were swallowed up
into the church. As the heavy doors closed behind me,
there was a sudden burden of breath upon my neck,
sweet and musty warm. The wind rose swirling snow
about my legs. The trees in the yard began to shake,
the brittle branches clacking together, clicking
together, clicking, click click, click click, click click.

Road Noise 1

The story of your skin echoes along the steel-ice rails
that run like black-blood veins over the heart of

America, shivers beneath the screeching wheels of lumbering engines. The rocking boxcars are haunted by the dreams you left behind, that howling. The freight yards ring with the ghost songs of men like you.

Men like you, who as boys, jumped the trains to escape the farmers and their fields, the forced labor, the hands that held the whips that burned the welts into your backs.

Men like you, who as boys, only a generation after Wounded Knee, a generation after the assassination of Sitting Bull, lived with all that blood screaming in your ears, all that blood running down your backs, all of that stinging.

Men like you, who as boys, grieved for the thunder of the herds, dreamed of the thunder of the ponies and their hooves, that howling.

Men like you, who as boys, sought out, discovered and created, road noise.

Fists and Fingers Dream

A man can be so many things, hard and cold and soft and warm and tender. A man can be smooth as a blade, jagged at the edge. His eyes can draw you in, cut you open wide to please his teeth. A man can be so many things, a sinner or a saint, anything that fists or fingers can dream.

The witnesses say, *The thing about him was his voice. Glory, he was angel-tongued. Devil, he was like*

Lucifer with that laugh that made you reach for a
rosary. He had the most gentle hands, stroking my
hair that day on the porch, humming one of them
Indian songs. He's the one, that's him, he was saying
candy and then his big hand was up and under and I...

When he caught that woman who jumped from the
window of the burning building, he was sixty years
old, got an award from the police. He hit that cop so
hard, even his wife, afterward, didn't recognize his
face. I saw him once empty his pockets to all those
drunks outside the tavern, gave 'em everything he had.
Two months with him and there was nothing left, but
us in the street, and him never looking back. My kids,
they loved him, jumped all up and down when he
came 'round. He slapped that little boy on the ass till
he was either gonna piss or bleed. Potty training. He
had it hard, you know, his mama saying he was
someone else's child, not even hers. He gave it hard,
you know, left behind so many bruises, so many
bodies, so much wreckage.

A man can be so many things, broken or beautiful,
strong or lonely. Damaged, damned and angry.
Resurrected. Forgiven or forgotten. A man can be so
many things, a sinner or a saint, anything that fists or
fingers can dream.

Road Noise 2

For men like you, the rhythm in the rails leads to the
hiss of desert highways laid out flat, edge of Earth to
edge of Earth, everything and nothing in-between.
From Flagstaff to Needles to Barstow, snapping lizard
tongues, dried up armadillos, the devil's playground,

everything and nothing in-between. Juke joints, truck stops, cup o' coffee cup o' coffee. Revival Lighthouse Palace of Christ, speak in tongues for a bowl o' soup bowl o' soup. You mop a floor, peel off a pair of fishnets, pick a pocket, and level that thumb again over the heated strip of tar and dreams, that howling.

Slice your way through the north-country, the hum of the roads walled in forests, far as the eye can see, tree line to tree line, everything and nothing in-between. From Duluth to Chicago to Detroit, belching factories, rotten-egg rivers, the rust-belt grind, everything and nothing in-between. Juke joints, truck stops, cup o' coffee cup o' coffee. Salvation Army bread lines, sing a hymn for a bowl o' soup bowl o' soup. You wash a dish, bust a head, then go to jail, listen to the wheels whining in your bones, that howling, father highway calling.

Election Day 2

As America was stirring from its usual slumber, I stood on the ice-encrusted steps of the church at St. Ann's Mission. I crushed the butt of my cigarette beneath the toe of my new dress shoe, tightened and straightened the knot of my tie and turned to enter into the church, into the dim light of death and murmuring. *There he is, that's Andrew's boy, don't you know he looks like Andy's boy.* As they all looked to me, searching my face for a sign, I nodded, floating between the pews. They all looked to me.

The long gray box was open and waiting at the other end of the room. The long gray box was open and vibrating at the other end of the room. The long gray box was open and laughing at the other end of the room. My hands began to remember. There once was a sunny day, big water.

Then, suddenly I was heavy to the floor, the aisle stretched out before me like another endless highway, a pavement hot and sticky with blood beneath my heels. My hands began. At the other end of the room the long gray box was open and spinning, the needle in a mad compass every direction pointing to every direction.

My hands, the box was open, began to remember, the box was open, I hated you, the box was open, I denied you, the box was open, I waited for you, the box was open, I looked for you, the box was open, I loved you, the box was open and spinning, and they were all looking to me, searching my face for a sign, and my hands began to remember.

Road Noise 3

Father highway calling, the wheels whining in your bones, everything and nothing in-between. Only the road noise in your head, your blood always remembering, your blood always reminding you there is no way to get away.

The story of your skin was written in the wind of wounded horses, and the world never wanted to hear that noise. The noise of men like you. The world didn't want to know and would not know and could not know. So, they give you thirty days in the hole, bread and water bread and water, over and over, again and again.

* * *

No, America doesn't want to hear that noise. They just want to make it, and louder. Their chugging engines to muffle the sound of their cannons. Their clanking factories to drown the sound of Chippewa children falling in the snow. The hiss of machines to bury the sound of bad medicine hidden in the weave of blankets. The boiling pots of rancid meat, the maggots twisting in a plate of beans, I mean, they don't want to hear. Not even the noise they make, the noise they gave to men like you.

The noise to be born with and raised with, to live with and to love with, to hurt with and hate with, create with and kill with. The noise of men like you pacing in your cells, rocking on your heels, shadowboxing, boxing all those shadows. Always in motion, always the father highway calling, always holding your hands over your ears, tearing at your hair, saying, *stop it stop it stop it, it hurts oh, God God God, it hurts, you hurt me, God, you hurt me, you let them hurt me with their God, with all that noise.*

The story of your skin is told in the rumblings that shiver through you, in the endless hall of echoes stretching through you like a road, winding deeper and deeper back into the forests of men like you, forests filled with the ghost songs of men like you. And through your blood, men like you, leave the noise to ring in the ears of men like me.

Dust

Little boys, they sure do love their daddies, look up to their daddies, they want to walk like their daddies, they want to talk like their daddies, too, they want to try their feet inside his shoes. Don't you know, they love to hear, *someday you're gonna be big just like your daddy*. Little boys, they love to fall into his wide grin, love to be lifted in his hands, higher than the trees. And they love to watch him dance with Mama, to hold her safe and tight, to listen to him hum and strum guitar, singing songs to Mama, just like Johnny Cash, singing, *flesh and blood needs flesh and blood, and you're the one I need.* Like Jim Reeves or Hank Locklin's "Four Walls," *out where the bright lights are glowing, you're drawn like a moth to a flame, you laugh while the wine's overflowing, while I sit and whisper your name.* Little boys, they sure do love their daddies.

The child was struck, at a tender age, with the dry mouth taste of his father's dust. The dust of lies, the dust of rage, the dust of wandering, the going away. The child was struck, gasping for air, parched and choking on the memory growing in his throat. For his father made the earth shudder beneath the fall of his foot. His father made other men tremble beneath the gust of his voice. The dust of lies, the dust of rage, the dust of wandering, the going away. For his father ate the sky with his teeth, and with his hands dragged deep scars into the flesh of hearts, the flesh of backs, the flesh of minds, into the flesh of dreams.

For his father was the first to bruise the child with the fist of his patience, to rape the child with the body of shame, to sting the child with the tongue of hate. The dust of lies, the dust of rage, the dust of wandering, the going away.

The child was struck, at a tender age, with the dry mouth taste of his father's dust, for his father was the first to make the child want to spit.

You laugh while the wine's overflowing, while I sit and whisper your name. Little boys, they sure do love their daddies, always trying to be like Daddy, trying to find Daddy in their own eyes. Always trying to find Daddy, to find Daddy, to find Daddy. And daddies, don't you know, they love their little boys.

Road Noise 4

Through your blood, men like you leave the noise to ring in the ears of men like me. And that's all you ever gave, that noise, taut wires snapping in my veins. All you ever gave to me is the need to kill the noise with more noise, to walk away and walk away, to heed the call of father highway, the call of highway father.

For you, the four walls were the four directions stretching endlessly, everything and nothing in-between. And I learned it right away. At three years old I hit the road, and when they realized I was gone, they caught up with me a mile and a half away, and I told them I was going to find my daddy, because I needed to find my daddy. When they realized I was gone.

Still, I swore I was never gonna be like you. But I was angry, I was hopeless. I couldn't touch, I couldn't feel anything or anyone. I swore I was never gonna be like you. But all the while my wheels were turning, I was on that road, spinning and spinning. I was thirteen and driving so fast and so far into my core that I saw nothing but the blur of passing landscapes. I was seventeen and driving so fast and so far out of myself that I knew nothing but pure light, a blinding light. I was twenty-five and driving, hit and run, leaving a few bodies behind, now. I was thirty and driving, leaving a few dreams behind, a little more of myself behind. And when they realized I was gone, caught up with me a lifetime and a half away, crawling along the shoulder of the road, I told them I was going to find my daddy, because I needed to find my daddy, to look into his eyes, to ask him, *why, why do I need to be like you?*

The Waiting

And while you were growing old in Fargo, I was growing weary. Waiting for you on the side of the road, waiting in those wide-open west-Texas nights. Even standing perfectly still, I answered the call of father highway, staring up at the stars, driving deeper and deeper into my own night, the Earth turning beneath me, the thundering herds, the ponies and their hooves, all that blood screaming in my ears, saying, *you are he you are he you are he.*

All that blood, my hands shaking, opening and closing, trying to reach out.

I was el Indio the night of the dance. Down along the border whirling, I watched her whirl to Tejano guitars, while golden beckoning birds flew from beneath her shimmering skirt.

* * *

My tequila fingers, reaching for her, trapped a bird within her hem, ripped the glimmering thread, and she looked at me as though I had torn the moonlight in half.

While you were dying in Fargo, I was exhausted. My hands empty, el Indio waiting on the side of the road, walking the mesquite desert, looking for any sign of my family, footprints, feathers, blood. My bones so noisy, now, that there was nothing but sound, white noise at fever pitch all those voices telling me, *you are he you are he.*

And then one night there was nothing left but the sputtering candle. The monster of my face in the bottom of the glass, the noise. The night the bullet the pistol the finger and the trigger, and me never looking back. I was el Indio, waiting for you to set me free, when the telephone rang. There was a whispering, saying, *you are he you are he you are he.*

Election Day 3

As America was stirring from its usual slumber, I was moving down the aisle of the church at St. Ann's Mission. They were all looking to me, searching my face for a sign. Before me, the long gray box was open and waiting.

My hands began to remember, the box was open and singing, my hands, the box was open and humming one of them Indian songs, my hands began, the box was open and whispering, and centuries began speaking to me —

Come closer, Grandson, they said, *we have been waiting for you, he has been waiting for you. It is time to begin to finish. It is time to break the circle, to make the circle new again. It is time to rise up from the father highway, to rise up and fly, for you are not he you are not he. It is time to bury the man, to find the father, even if a father he could never be. It is time to make it so, to set yourself free, for you are not he you are not he.*

The box was open and waiting. I saw you. It was election day and my hands began to remember.

Hands

Old man, I stood over you in your box, and when I reached to touch your gray folded hands I remembered, instantly, a fair summer day beside big water, when you laughed and lifted me higher than the trees, and I felt like a big boy, I felt like a big boy, in your hands I felt like a good boy, and you said, *hey Chee-pwa, do you see any angels up there, do you see any angels up there?*

Old man, I leaned over you in your box, touched my hands into your thin gray wave of hair and I whispered, may the Grandfathers give you feathers, all is forgiven down here...

"Road Noise" is included in *Exploding Chippewas*, TriQuarterly Books/Northwestern University Press, 2002.

Remarks
Chris Hedges

Remarks by the President on Review of Signals Intelligence
(if he had told the truth)
Department of Injustice
Washington, D.C.
11:15 a.m. EST

THE PRESIDENT: A small, secret surveillance committee of goons and thugs hiding behind the mask of patriotism was established in 1908 in Washington, D.C. The group was led from 1924 until 1972 by J. Edgar Hoover, and during his reign it became known as the Federal Bureau of Investigation. FBI agents spied upon and infiltrated labor unions, political parties, radical groups—especially those led by African-Americans—anti-war groups and the civil rights movement in order to discredit anyone, including politicians such as Henry Wallace, who questioned the power of the state and big business. Agents burglarized homes and offices, illegally opened mail and planted unlawful wiretaps. Bureau leaders created blacklists. They destroyed careers and sometimes lives. They demanded loyalty oaths. By the time they were done, our progressive and radical movements, which had given us the middle class and opened up our political system, were dead. And while the FBI was targeting internal dissidents, our foreign intelligence operatives were overthrowing regimes, bankrolling some of the most vicious dictators on the planet and carrying out assassinations in numerous countries, such as Cuba and the Philippines and later Iran, Guatemala, Vietnam, Chile, Iraq and Afghanistan.

Throughout American history, intelligence services often did little more than advance and protect corporate profits and solidify state repression and imperialist expansion. War, for big business, has always been very lucrative and used as an excuse to curtail basic liberties and crush popular movements. "Inter arma silent leges," as Cicero said, or "During war, the laws are silent." In the Civil War, during which the North and the South suspended the writ of habeas corpus and up to 750,000 soldiers died in the slaughter, Union intelligence worked alongside Northern war profiteers who sold cardboard shoes to the Army as the spy services went about the business of ruthlessly hunting down deserters. The First World War, which gave us the Espionage Act and the Sedition Act and saw President Woodrow Wilson throw populists and socialists, including Socialist leader Eugene V. Debs, into prison, produced $28.5 billion in net profits for businesses and created 22,000 new millionaires. Wall Street banks, which lent $2.5 billion to nations allied with the United States, made sure Wilson sent U.S. forces into the senseless trench warfare so they would be repaid. World War II—which consumed more than 50 million lives and saw 110,000 Japanese-Americans hauled away to internment camps and atomic bombs dropped on defenseless civilians—doubled wartime corporate profits from the First World War. Why disarm when there was so much money to be made from stoking fear?

* * *

The rise of the Iron Curtain and nuclear weapons provided the justification by big business for sustaining a massive arms industry, for a huge expansion of our surveillance capabilities and for more draconian assaults against workers and radicals. The production of weapons was about profits rather than logic. We would go on to produce more than 70,000 nuclear bombs or warheads at a cost of $5.5 trillion, enough weapons to obliterate every Soviet city several times over. And in the early days of the Cold War, with Hoover and Joe McCarthy and his henchmen blacklisting anyone with a conscience in government, the arts, journalism, labor unions or education, President Harry S. Truman created the National Security Agency, or NSA.

Throughout this evolution, Americans were steadily shorn of their most basic constitutional rights and their traditions of limited government. U.S. intelligence agencies were always anchored in a system of secrecy—with little effective oversight from either elected leaders or ordinary citizens. Meanwhile, totalitarian states like East Germany offered a sterling example of what our corporate masters might achieve with pervasive, unchecked surveillance that turned citizens into informers and persecuted people for what they said in the privacy of their homes. Today I would like to thank the architects of this East German system, especially Erich Mielke, once the chief of the communist East German secret police. I want to assure them that the NSA has gone on to perfect what the Stasi began.

* * *

In the 1960s, the U.S. government spied on civil rights leaders, the Black Panthers, the American Indian Movement and critics of the Vietnam War, just as today we are spying on Occupy activists, environmentalists, whistle-blowers and other dissidents. And partly in response to these revelations decades ago, especially regarding the FBI's covert dirty tricks program known as COINTELPRO, laws were established in the 1970s to ensure that our intelligence capabilities could not be misused against our citizens. In the long, twilight struggle against communism, and now in the fight against terrorism, I am happy to report that we have eradicated all of these reforms and laws. The crimes for which Richard Nixon resigned and the abuses of power that prompted the formation of the Church Commission are now legal. The liberties that some patriots, including Daniel Ellsberg, Chelsea Manning and Edward Snowden, have sought to preserve have been sacrificed at the altar of national security. To obtain your personal information, the FBI can now freely issue "national security letters" to your bank, doctor, employer or public library or any of your associates without a judicial warrant. And you will never be notified of an investigation. We can collect and store in perpetuity all metadata of your email correspondence and phone records and track your geographical movements. We can assassinate you if I decide you are a terrorist. We can order the military under Section 1021 of the National Defense Authorization Act to arrest you, strip you of due process and hold you indefinitely in military detention centers. We can continue to throw into prison those who expose the illegality of what we are doing, or force them into exile, as all totalitarian secret police forces from the SS to the KGB to the East German Stasi have done. And we can torture.

* * *

The fall of the Soviet Union left America without a competing superpower. This threatened to delegitimize our massive spending on war and state security, now more than 50 percent of our budget. But a group of Islamic radicals who had never posed an existential threat to our country emerged to take the place of the old communist bloc. The politics of fear and the psychosis of permanent war were able to be continued. The war on terror placed new and in some ways more complicated demands on our intelligence agencies. Our illegal and disastrous occupations of Iraq and Afghanistan and our indiscriminate bombing of other countries, along with the war crimes Israel is carrying out against the Palestinian people, are driving people in the Muslim world into the arms of these militant groups. We are the most hated nation on earth. At the same time, globalization—our corporate policy of creating a worldwide neofeudalism of masters and serfs—means we must spy on citizens to prevent agitation and revolt. After all, if you are a worker, things are only going to get worse. To quash competitors of American companies, we spy on corporations in Brazil, including Brazil's biggest oil company, Petrobras, and on corporations in Germany and France. We also steal information from the leaders of many countries, including German Chancellor Angela Merkel, whose personal cellphone we tapped. However, Ms. Merkel, who grew up in East Germany, should not, as she has done, accuse us of being the Stasi. We are much more efficient than the Stasi was. We spied successfully on U.N. Secretary-General Ban Ki-moon, in addition to Pope Francis and the conclave that elected him last March. Senior U.N. officials and Roman Catholic cardinals are highly susceptible to recruitment by al-Qaida. The reasons are classified. I won't share them with you. Believe me.

Threats to the nation raised new legal and policy questions, which fortunately our courts, abject tools of the corporate state, solved by making lawful everything from torture to wholesale surveillance. I would like to take a moment to thank our nation's compliant judges, the spineless deans of most prestigious law schools and most law professors and lawyers for refusing to defend the Constitution. They have been valued partners, along with the press, in our campaign to eradicate your civil liberties.

The horror of September 11th was masterfully manipulated by the security state and our for-profit military-industrial complex. These forces used the attacks as an excuse to increase the massive pilfering of taxpayer dollars, especially by the Department of Homeland Security, which has a public budget of $98.8 billion. The truth, however, is the system of internal security is so vast and so secret no one in the public has any idea how large our programs are or how much we spend. It is true that our 16 intelligence agencies missed the numerous signs and evidence leading up to the 9/11 attacks. In short, they screwed up, just as they did when they failed to anticipate the fall of the Shah of Iran or the collapse of the Soviet Union, or when they told us Saddam Hussein had weapons of mass destruction. But we have a rule in Washington: Never reform failed bureaucracies or hold government officials accountable; rather, give them more money. Keep failure secret.

It is a testimony to the hard work and dedication of the men and women of our intelligence community that over the past decade we've taken enormous strides in making the Middle East a cauldron of rage. New capabilities and new laws have turned us into the most efficient killers on the planet. Relationships with foreign intelligence services have expanded, creating one immense, global corporate system of surveillance and security that obliterates the rights of people at home and abroad. Taken together, these efforts have killed hundreds of thousands of innocents in Iraq, Afghanistan, Pakistan, Somalia and Yemen. We have terrorized whole countries from the sky and forced millions to become refugees. This will ensure endless war, which ensures endless profits for those who make war—which is the point.

Over the last six months, I created an outside Review Group on Intelligence and Communications Technologies to make recommendations for reform. This group is led by the same intelligence chiefs who carry out the abuses. The chancellor of Germany has, like many of our other allies, demanded we stop spying on citizens of that nation. But, unfortunately for the chancellor, as well as for you, my fellow Americans, we will continue to do whatever we want.

The folks at the NSA and other intelligence agencies are our nation's voyeurs and peeping Toms. They read your electronic bank and medical records. They know what you and your kids post on Facebook and Instagram. They have all of your emails and text messages. They track your movements through the GPS on your cellphone. They are not alone. Corporations of all kinds and sizes track your online searches and what you buy, then they analyze and store the data and use it for commercial purposes; that's why those targeted ads pop up on your computer and your smartphone so often.

Given the unique power of the state, it is not enough for leaders to say "trust us, we won't abuse the data we collect." History has too many examples of such trust being breached. Our system of government is built on the premise that our liberty cannot depend on the good intentions of those in power; it depends on the law to constrain those in power. And that is why Congress and our courts have rewritten our laws, from the NDAA to the FISA Amendment Act, to strip you of legal protection.

I would not be where I am today were it not for the courage of dissidents like Martin Luther King Jr. who were spied upon by their own government. But I, like Bill Clinton, have sold out those true patriots and gutted those government programs that made possible my own education and ascent into systems of elite power. As president I understand, as do Bill and Hillary, that political power is about us, not about you. I know where power in this country lies. It does not lie with the citizen. It lies with Wall Street and corporate boardrooms. And since my vanity demands that I be famous, wealthy and powerful, I work hard for these centers of power. None of these centers of power want to see any curbs on the security and surveillance state. And so I will make sure there are none.

As a senator, I was critical of practices such as warrantless wiretaps. But as president I have carried out a far more extensive assault on civil liberties than my predecessor, George W. Bush. I have used the Espionage Act eight times to charge patriots such as Edward Snowden who exposed crimes of the state.

And I have lied to you often, as I did in the original version of this speech, to defend the right of our security and surveillance apparatus to spy on you without judicial warrants.

As a presidential candidate in 2008 I promised to "reject the use of national security letters to spy on citizens who are not suspected of a crime." I promised to close our detention center in Guantanamo Bay. I said I would revisit the Patriot Act. I told you I would overturn unconstitutional executive decisions issued by the Bush administration. I said I would shut down our black sites. And I promised an end to extraordinary rendition. I told you as president last summer that the NSA "cannot target your emails" and that all of our surveillance programs were subject to the full control of Congress. I have, along with our Congress and our highest courts, eradicated the Fourth Amendment, which once protected citizens from government intrusion into their persons, homes, papers and effects. And, to be frank, the only reason I am talking to you today about spying is because Edward Snowden has, through his leaked documents, illustrated that everything I and others in government have promised to do or told you about domestic and international surveillance is a lie.

Today I am announcing a series of cosmetic reforms that my administration intends to adopt administratively or will seek to codify through Congress.

First, I have approved a new presidential directive for our signals intelligence activities both at home and abroad that sounds impressive but means nothing.

* * *

Second, we will institute a few bureaucratic programs and procedures to give you the illusion of greater transparency while we continue to sweep up and store your personal information, including your telephone metadata.

Third, I propose more amorphous and undefined protections for government activities conducted under Section 702.

Fourth, the FBI's national security letters will not be touched. But we could and should be more transparent in how government uses this authority. We really should. But we won't. To make you feel better, however, I have directed the attorney general to amend how we use national security letters so that this secrecy will not be indefinite, so that it will terminate within a fixed—though unspecified—time unless the government demonstrates a need for further secrecy. That need might last forever.

This brings me to the program that has generated the most controversy these past few months—the bulk collection of telephone records under Section 215. Why is this necessary? It is necessary because in a totalitarian state the secret police must gather information not to solve crimes but, as Hannah Arendt pointed out, "to be on hand when the government decides to arrest a certain category of the population." We need all of your emails, phone conversations, Web searches and geographical movements for "evidence" should we decide to seize you. And my apologies to Sen. Bernie Sanders, but we can't make exemptions for members of Congress, especially when they come from Vermont. If you think you are innocent, or that you have nothing to hide, you do not understand what is happening. Justice, like truth, is no longer relevant. Ask Chelsea Manning, Julian Assange or Edward Snowden, along with whistle-blowers like Thomas Drake, where justice and truth got them. One of the main tasks of any security service is blackmail, a tactic the FBI used to try to get Martin Luther King to commit suicide. So if you have any dirt we want to know about it.

I will propose turning over the storage of all your data to a third party, perhaps a private corporation. This will offer you no protection, but it should provide a good government contract to one of my major campaign donors.

The cosmetic reforms I'm proposing today will, I hope, give the American people greater confidence that their rights are being protected, even as our intelligence and law enforcement agencies, along with our courts, continue to eviscerate those rights. I recognize that there are additional issues that require further debate, such as your constitutional right to halt the wholesale capturing and storing of your personal information and correspondence and evidence of your geographical movements. But don't expect me to help. I sold out long ago.

The bottom line is that people around the world, regardless of their nationality, can be assured that the United States follows everything they do or say. It does not matter if they are ordinary people or foreign leaders. I am not going to apologize for monitoring the communications of friends and allies. We know what we are doing. We know why this is important.

The effects of declining incomes for working men and women, the massive debt peonage that keeps people trapped, the slashing of government assistance programs, the chronic, long-term unemployment, and the effects of climate change will eventually trigger volatile unrest. We are ready. The likelihood of totalitarianism no longer comes from fascism or communism. It comes from corporations. Corporations, for which I work, fear those who think and write and speak out and form relationships freely. Individual freedom impedes their profits. And the surveillance system I am protecting today is designed to keep these corporations in power.

Our democracy is a fiction. We seek to maintain this fiction to keep you passive. Should you wake up, we will not shy away from draconian measures. I believe we can meet high expectations. Together, let us chart a way forward that secures your complete subjugation, the iron rule of our corporations and our power elite—at least until we make the planet wholly uninhabitable—while we continue to snuff out the liberties that once made our nation worth fighting for.

Thank you. May God bless you. May God bless Corporate America.

"Remarks" by Chris Hedges first appeared on Truthdig.com.

One Stick Song
Sherman Alexie

and so now, near the end of the game
when I only have one stick left to lose

and so now, near the end of the game
when I only have one stick left to lose

I will sing a one-stick song
I will sing a one-stick song

to bring back all the other sticks
to bring back all the other sticks

I will sing of my uncle
and the vein that burst in his head

o, bright explosion, crimson and magenta
o, kind uncle, brown skin and white T-shirt

o, crimson, magenta
o, brown, white

o, crimson
o, brown

o, uncle, kind uncle
I sing you back, I sing you back

and I will sing of my cousin
who jumped off the bridge

o, bright explosion, crimson and magenta
o, falling cousin, pink marrow and white water

o, crimson, magenta
o, pink, white

o, crimson
o, pink

o, cousin, falling cousin
I sing you back, I sing you back

and I will sing of my grandfather
killed by the sniper on Okinawa

o, bright explosion, crimson and magenta
o, soldier grandfather, green uniform and white sand

o, crimson, magenta
o, green, white

o, crimson
o, green

o, grandfather, soldier grandfather
I sing you back, I sing you back

and I will sing of the uncle
crushed beneath the fallen tree

o, bright explosion, crimson and magenta
o, small uncle, silver axe and white wood

o, crimson, magenta
o, silver, white

o, crimson
o, silver

o, uncle, small uncle
I sing you back, I sing you back

and I will sing of my grandmother
and her lover called tuberculosis

o, bright explosion, crimson and magenta
o, coughing grandmother, red blood and white
handkerchief

o, crimson, magenta
o, red, white

o, crimson
o, red

o, grandmother, coughing grandmother
I sing you back, I sing you back

and I will sing of my aunt
who looked back and turned into a pillar of sugar

o, bright explosion, crimson and magenta
o, diabetic aunt, yellow skin and white tower

o, crimson, magenta
o, yellow, white

o, crimson
o, yellow

o, aunt, diabetic aunt
I sing you back, I sing you back

and I will sing of my cousin
who hitchhiked over the horizon

o, bright explosion, crimson and magenta
o, lost cousin, turquoise ring and white scar

o, crimson, magenta
o, turquoise, white

o, crimson
o, turquoise

o, cousin, lost cousin
I sing you back, I sing you back

and I will sing of my sister
asleep when her trailer burned

o, bright explosion, crimson and magenta
o, burned sister, scarlet skin and white ash

o, crimson, magenta
o, scarlet, white

o, crimson
o, scarlet

o, sister, burned sister
I sing you back, I sing you back

and I will sing of my uncle
and his lover called cirrhosis

o, bright explosion, crimson and magenta
o, swollen uncle, black liver and white hair

o, crimson, magenta
o, black, white

o, crimson
o, black

o, uncle, swollen uncle
I sing you back, I sing you back

and I will sing of my grandmother
heavy with tumors

o, bright explosion, crimson and magenta
o, big grandmother, gold uranium and white X-ray

o, crimson, magenta
o, gold, white

o, crimson
o, gold

o, grandmother, big grandmother
I sing you back, I sing you back

and I will sing of my cousin
shot in the head by a forgetful man

o, bright explosion, crimson and magenta
o, drunk cousin, gray matter and white bone

o, crimson, magenta
o, gray, white

o, crimson
o, gray

o, cousin, drunk cousin
I sing you back, I sing you back

I sing you back, I sing all of you back
I sing you back, I sing all of you back

I sing you back from the parking lot of the convenience store
I sing you back from the sixth floor of the Catholic hospital
I sing you back from the seventh floor of the Veterans Hospital
back from the floor of your trailer house
from the cold fog of San Francisco
from 544 East Dave Court
I sing you back from the blood-stained wall
from the stand of pine
the Pacific Ocean
the Spokane River
I sing you back from Chimacum Creek.

I sing you back, I sing all of you back
I sing you back, I sing all of you back

and so now, near the end of the game
when I only have one stick left to win with

and so now, near the end of the game
when I only have one stick left to win with

I will sing a one-stick song
I will sing a one-stick song

to celebrate all of my sticks
returned to me

to celebrate all of my sticks
returned to me

returned to me
returned to me

returned to me
returned to me

ABOUT THE CONTRIBUTORS

Sherman Alexie has won the National Book Award. He is the author of twenty-four books to date.

Esther G. Belin was raised in Lynwood, California. She is the author of *From the Belly of My Beauty*.

Dickey Betts is a musician and songwriter from Florida. He is a member of the Rock and Roll Hall of Fame and has played on numerous albums.

Ron Cooper is the author of the novels *Hume's Fork*, *Purple Jesus*, and the forthcoming *Gospel of the Twin*.

Patrick Michael Finn is the author of a short story collection and a novella. He lives in Arizona.

Larry Fondation is the author two novels and three short story collections. His fiction focuses primarily on the Los Angeles underbelly.

Michael Gills is author of *Why I Lie, Go Love, The Death of Bonnie and Clyde*, and *White Indians*.

Joseph D. Haske is a writer, critic and scholar, whose debut novel, *North Dixie Highway*, was released in October 2013.

William Hastings, editor, is the author of *The Hard Way.* He works as a farmhand and as a bookseller.

Chris Hedges is a senior fellow at The Nation Institute and a columnist for *Truthdig.* He is the author of numerous books.

Vicki Hendricks is the author of five novels including *Miami Purity* and Edgar Finalist *Cruel Poetry.* Her newest novel is *Fur People.*

Steven Huff is the author of a collection of short stories and two books of poems. He is the founder of Tiger Bark Press.

Jason Isbell is a musician and songwriter from Alabama. He has six albums.

Chris Offutt is the author of five books and ten screenplays. Forthcoming in 2015 is his memoir *A Desk, a Rifle, and Eighteen Hundred Pounds of Porn.*

Mark Turcotte (Turtle Mountain Chippewa) lives in Chicago, where he teaches in the English Department at DePaul University.

Willy Vlautin has written four novels and is a member of the band Richmond Fontaine.

Eric Miles Williamson is author of four books of fiction and three books of criticism. His works have been translated and published internationally.

Daniel Woodrell lives on the Missouri side of the Arkansas line. He has published nine novels and a collection of short stories.

OTHER TITLES FROM DOWN AND OUT BOOKS

See www.DownAndOutBooks.com for complete list

By Anonymous-9
Bite Hard

By J.L. Abramo
Catching Water in a Net
Clutching at Straws
Counting to Infinity
Gravesend
Chasing Charlie Chan
Circling the Runway (*)

By Trey R. Barker
2,000 Miles to Open Road
Road Gig: A Novella
Exit Blood
Death is Not Forever (*)

By Richard Barre
The Innocents
Bearing Secrets
Christmas Stories
The Ghosts of Morning
Blackheart Highway
Burning Moon
Echo Bay
Lost

By Eric Beetner and
JB Kohl
Over Their Heads (*)

By Eric Beetner and
Frank Scalise
The Backlist (*)

By Rob Brunet
Stinking Rich

By Milton T. Burton
Texas Noir

By Dana Cameron (editor)
Murder at the Beach:
Bouchercon Anthology 2014

By Tom Crowley
Vipers Tail
Murder in the Slaughterhouse

By Frank De Blase
Pine Box for a Pin-Up
Busted Valentines and Other
Dark Delights
A Cougar's Kiss (*)

By Les Edgerton
The Genuine, Imitation,
Plastic Kidnapping

By A.C. Frieden
Tranquility Denied
The Serpent's Game
The Pyongyang Option (*)

By Jack Getze
Big Numbers
Big Money
Big Mojo

(*)—Coming Soon

OTHER TITLES FROM DOWN AND OUT BOOKS

See www.DownAndOutBooks.com for complete list

By Keith Gilman
Bad Habits

By William Hastings (editor)
*Stray Dogs: Writing from
the Other America*

By Matt Hilton
No Going Back (*)
Rules of Honor (*)
The Lawless Kind (*)

By Terry Holland
An Ice Cold Paradise
Chicago Shiver

By Darrel James,
Linda O. Johnston
& Tammy Kaehler (editors)
Last Exit to Murder

By David Housewright
& Renée Valois
The Devil and the Diva

By David Housewright
Finders Keepers
Full House

By Jon Jordan
Interrogations

By Jon & Ruth Jordan (editors)
*Murder and Mayhem in
Muskego*

By Bill Moody
Czechmate
The Man in Red Square
Solo Hand
The Death of a Tenor Man
The Sound of the Trumpet
Bird Lives!

By Gary Phillips
The Perpetrators
Scoundrels (Editor)
Treacherous

By Gary Phillips, Tony Chavira
& Manoel Maglhaes
Beat L.A. (Graphic Novel)

By Robert J. Randisi
Upon My Soul
Souls of the Dead (*)
Envy the Dead (*)

By Lono Waiwaiole
Wiley's Lament
Wiley's Shuffle
Wiley's Refrain
Dark Paradise

By Vincent Zandri
Moonlight Weeps

(*)—Coming Soon

Made in the USA
San Bernardino, CA
05 December 2016